Shirley Q...

Praise for

LARRY McMURTRY

"McMurtry can transform ordinary words into highly lyrical, poetic passages. . . . He presents human dramas with a sympathy and compassion that makes us care about his characters in ways that most novelists can't."

—*Los Angeles Times*

"Mr. McMurtry's characters are real, believable and touching. His prose has life and immediacy . . . always a delight to read."

—*The New York Times Book Review*

"McMurtry writes beautifully. . . ."

—*Alabama Journal*

"Mr. McMurtry is blessed with an absolutely solid sense of place. His backgrounds and scenic descriptions are inherent parts of his story, contributing as much to the novel as does the completely natural dialogue."

—*Saturday Review*

"McMurtry is among the most imaginative writers working today."

—*San Francisco Chronicle*

Books by Larry McMurtry

Buffalo Girls
Some Can Whistle
Anything for Billy
Film Flam: Essays on Hollywood
Texasville
Lonesome Dove
The Desert Rose
Cadillac Jack
Somebody's Darling
Terms of Endearment
All My Friends Are Going to Be Strangers
Moving On
The Last Picture Show
In a Narrow Grave: Essays on Texas
Leaving Cheyenne
Horseman, Pass By

Most Pocket Books are available at special quantity discounts for bulk purchases for sales promotions, premiums or fund raising. Special books or book excerpts can also be created to fit specific needs.

For details write the office of the Vice President of Special Markets, Pocket Books, 1230 Avenue of the Americas, New York, New York 10020.

Shirley Quincy

LARRY McMURTRY

Horseman, Pass By

POCKET BOOKS

New York   London   Toronto   Sydney   Tokyo   Singapore

This book is a work of fiction. Names, characters, places and incidents are either products of the author's imagination or are used fictitiously. Any resemblance to actual events or locales or persons, living or dead, is entirely coincidental.

POCKET BOOKS, a division of Simon & Schuster Inc.
1230 Avenue of the Americas, New York, NY 10020

Copyright © 1961 by Larry McMurtry
Copyright renewed © 1989 by Larry McMurtry

Published by arrangement with the author

All rights reserved, including the right to reproduce
this book or portions thereof in any form whatsoever.
For information address Pocket Books, 1230 Avenue
of the Americas, New York, NY 10020

ISBN: 0-671-75384-3

First Pocket Books printing June 1992

10 9 8 7 6 5 4 3 2 1

POCKET and colophon are registered trademarks of
Simon & Schuster Inc.

Cover art by Earl Keleny

Printed in the U.S.A.

Dedicated to my parents,
W. J. and Hazel Ruth McMurtry,
with gratitude and love

Horseman, Pass By

PROLOGUE

LONNIE:

I remember how green the early oat fields were, that year, and how the plains looked in April, after the mesquite leafed out. Spring had come dry for seven straight years, and Granddad and the other cattlemen in Dry Bean County had had to watch the bare spots widening in their pastures. But that year the month of March was a long slow drizzle, and when it ended, the bare spots shrunk again and new grass carpeted the flats. When I rode out with him on Saturdays, Granddad would sometimes get down from his horse, to show me how the grass was shooting its runners over the droughty ground; and he told me that nature would always work her own cures, if people would be patient enough, and give her time. After school on the weekdays, riding the long road home through the ranches in the old yellow school bus, I watched the range change. I watched the whole ranch country shake off its dust and come alive.

At night, when the milking was done and the supper eaten, we sat on the east porch, in the late spring dusk, resting and talking about the day. On the warmest nights Grandma came out too, and rocked for a while in the cord-bottomed porch rocker, sometimes crocheting doilies to spread on the living room chairs. Even Hud might sit on the steps a few minutes, brushing his red suede boots before he left for town. But soon he would leave in his rag-topped Ford, and Grandma would get too cool and go back to her radio. Granddad and I sat on the porch alone, through the best hour—that last little while when he and I watched another day turning into night.

Just before full dark, the bull bats came out from somewhere and swooped around the lilac bushes; and the horses clopped past the yard on their way to the dark grazing flats below the hill. A highway ran alongside the horse pasture, a mile to the east of our house, and from the porch we could watch the cars zoom across the plains—north to Amarillo or Raton, south to Dallas or Houston or Fort Worth. The big Diesel trucks growled through the thick prairie dusk. The railroad was just the other side of the highway, and about sundown the Katy freight chugged by, pulling its string of oil and cattle cars. During the shipping season the cars were full of calves, their bawling a lonesome sound at twilight. Sometimes the bawling stirred Granddad: reminded him of other times he had heard it, and of men he had heard it with. Then he might tell me stories of his days on the big ranches, or of cowboys like his dead foreman Jericho Green. I sat below him, flipping my pocketknife into the soft dirt of Grandma's lilac beds, taking in every word he said.

Granddad was an old man then, and he worked hard days. By eight or eight-fifteen he was tired of sitting up. Around that time the nightly Zephyr flew by, blowing its loud whistle to warn the station men in Thalia. The noise cut across the dark prairie like the whistling train itself. I could see the hundred lighted windows of the passenger cars, and I wondered where in the world the people behind them were going night after night. To me it was exciting to think about a train. But the Zephyr blowing by seemed to make Granddad tireder; it seemed to make him sad. He told me one time that it reminded him of nights on roundup, long years ago. On quiet nights he and the other cowboys would sit around the fires, telling stories or drawing brands in the dirt. Some nights they would camp close to a railroad track, and a train would go by and blow its whistle at the fires. Sometimes it scared the cattle, and sometimes it didn't, but it always took the spirit out of the cowboys' talk; made them lonesomer than they could say. It made them think about womenfolk and fun and city lights till they could barely stand it. And long years after, when the last train would go by, Granddad got restless. He would stretch, and push

*his old rope-bottomed chair up against the house.
"Train's gone, son," he said to me. "It's bedtime."
Then he took his coffee-can spittoon over to the yard
fence, stood there long enough to piss, and went into
the house.*

*With that Granddad's day ended, and my night
really began. I went to the windmill and let the
faucet run till the coldest deep well water came
gurgling up through the pipes. After I drank I
sometimes went over and sat in the rope swing that
hung from the biggest sycamore limb, to drag my
feet in the sandy dirt and watch Granddad through
his window as he got ready for bed. When he had his
nightshirt on he usually came to stand awhile by the
window screen, looking into the dark and scratching
the scarred old leg that he had almost torn off in a
roping accident. Then he would turn his back on the
night, and go to bed.*

*When I knew Granddad was in bed I went back to
the windmill and stopped the blades, so I could
climb up and sit on the platform beneath the big fin.
Around me, across the dark prairie, the lights were
clear. The oil derricks were lit with strings of yellow
bulbs, like Christmas trees. The lights were still on in
the kitchens of the pumpers' cabins, the little green-
topped shacks scattered across the plain, each one
propped on a few stacks of bricks. Twelve miles
away, to the north, the red and green and yellow
lights of Thalia shimmered against the dark. I sat
above it all, in the cool breezy air that swept under*

the windmill blades, hearing the rig motors purr and the heavy trucks growl up the hill. Above the chattering of the ignorant Rhode Island Reds I heard two whippoorwills, the ghostly birds I never saw, calling across the flats below the ridge.

Sitting there with only the wind and the darkness around me, I thought of all the important things I had to think about: my honors, my worries, my ambitions. I thought of the wild nights ahead, when I would have my own car, and could tear across the country to dances and rodeos. I picked the boys I would run with, the girls we would romp; I kept happy thinking of all the reckless things that could happen in the next few years. Some nights it stormed out on the range, and I watched the little snake-tongues of lightning flicker against the clouds. When it was clear enough, I could see the airplane beacons flashing from the airport in Wichita Falls.

Later, I climbed down and drank from the faucet before I went to bed. I tiptoed through the kitchen, across the patches of moonlight that sometimes lay on the cool linoleum, and climbed the stairs to my room under the roof. On nights when I was wide awake I lay on top of the covers and read a paperback until I got drowsy, or until I heard Hud coming back from town. I was always ready to sleep by the time he came in. In the summers I slept with my head toward the foot of the bed, so I could see the moon and the yard trees out the window. That way I got what breeze there was; and that way, too, I only had to raise up on one elbow in the mornings to watch the lots, and see Granddad and the cowboys catching their horses for the new day. I didn't always sleep the hours a growing boy was supposed to, but the nights that spring were a field that I left well sown.

CHAPTER
1

For dessert that night Halmea made a big freezerful of peach ice cream, rich as Jersey milk and thick with hunks of sweet, lockerplant Albertas. It had for me the good, special flavor of something seasonal, something you have waited all winter to taste, like early roasting ears or garden tomatoes. I ate three big helpings and still couldn't get enough. When the freezer was almost empty I went in to get the dasher, but Hud shoved me out of the way and took it himself. We dished the last peachy drops of cream and took our bowls out on the porch to scrape them dry.

Granddad had taken his last helping of cream and gone out before us, and his empty blue saucer was sitting by his elbow when we came out. He sat on the bottom step of the porch, whittling on a cedar stick he had picked up that day. He whittled it down patiently, setting his knife in the reddish wood just so; and while I scraped my saucer I watched the thin slivers curl off the stick and drop between his legs. Eighty years old and more, Granddad was then, but the sandy hair on his head was still thick as ever, and his gray eyes were still steady and clear. He pulled the thin blade of the case knife in toward him, his mouth loosening as he worked. For a few minutes he went on smoothing the stick, and nothing was said. We all sat enjoying the quiet evening. Then Granddad looked up from his whittling and nodded toward the three empty bowls.

"Why don't you take them bowls in to Halmea?" he said to me. "She might want to get her dishes done."

"Then let the nigger bitch gather 'em up herself," Hud said. He sat on the edge of the porch, picking his teeth with a sharpened matchstick. He had on his suede boots and a new pearl-buttoned shirt, but he didn't seem to be in any hurry to leave for wherever he was going.

"Let her work a little," he said. "She sits on her butt all day."

"She ain't the only one," Granddad said, rubbing his fingers over the smooth length of stick. "It won't hurt Lonnie to move once in a while. He's young and supple."

"Young and simple," Hud said, spitting. He smirked at me when he said it, a lock of his dark crow hair falling over his forehead.

I got up and grabbed the three empty bowls and

took them in with no argument. Hud was thirty-five to my seventeen, and my best bet was to pay him as little mind as possible. Everybody in the county, even Granddad, took a little of Hud's sourness, and nobody felt quite big enough to do anything about it. Granddad kept him on partly because he was a stepson, I guess, and partly because, when Hud was interested and cared to be, he was as good as the best and more reckless than the wildest of the thousand wild-ass cowboys in the Texas cattle country.

When I went in with the bowls, Halmea was sitting by the kitchen table reading *True Romances*. The supper dishes were piled on the washboard, and the ice-cream freezer still stood in the sink. Hud was right about Halmea sitting on her butt nine tenths of the time, but she could afford to. She was the only one of us who could keep Grandma in a halfway good humor.

"You better get those dishes washed," I said. "Granny'll have kittens."

She looked up from the magazine, grinning her lazy, big-mouthed grin. "Few kittens jus' what she need," she said. "She worried so 'bout goin' to de hos-pital, she ain't gonna mind no dishes tonight. Get on an' let me read."

I sat the saucers in the sink and went down the darkened hall to the bathroom. When I came out, Grandma was standing by her bedroom door, looking for someone to pester.

"Lordy ain't it hot tonight," she said. "Help me

9

out on the porch and I'll sit awhile. My kidneys don't give me a minute's peace."

I took her arm and led her out to the rocking chair, but then I went back to the kitchen to keep from having to listen to her gripe. Halmea had laid her magazine down and was giving her toenails their daily coat from a bottle of nail polish she kept in the cabinet. Her big tan-soled feet were bare, one of them propped on the churn stool so she could reach her toes. She looked up suddenly and caught me glancing at her where her floppy blue dress was lifted off one leg; she just gave me that slow grin of hers and went back to dipping the toenail brush. "Tend you own rat-killin'," she said. I fiddled with the water pitcher a minute and decided I'd be just as well off listening to Grandma after all. Sometimes Halmea was too unconscious even to pester. I set the pitcher down and went back to the porch.

Grandma was wadding her calico apron between her hands and rocking like sixty, talking a blue streak to keep time with her rocking. "I never had no kidney operation," she said. "I hate to just lay there knocked out an' not keep up with what they're adoin' to me. I ought to be the one to say."

Over to the east, I saw a pickup pull off the highway and start across the dirt road toward us. "Here comes Jesse," I said. "I guess he got 'em unloaded."

He was a new hand, Jesse. Just a week before he had stepped off a cattle truck and come walking up

10

to the ranch house with nothing but a saddle and a paper sack full of clothes, looking for a job. Hud was against him from the minute he came through the gate, but Hud was against hiring anybody, and Granddad took Jesse on anyway. He was coming back from hauling a few dry cows to a new pasture; coming home to cold supper and no peach ice cream.

"I swan," Grandma said. "It's a pity an old woman like me has got to be cut into afore she dies. But it ain't aworryin' you-all one bit. They could cut off my nose an' nobody but me 'ud miss it. It's awful when an old woman can't get no sympathy from her own kinfolks."

"You're gonna get your bills paid, though," Hud said. "If I could accomplish that, they could have my nose." He laughed lazily, without looking at Grandma, and she began to daub at her eyes with the apron. I walked over to the north edge of the porch and looked off toward Thalia. Around us, under the last daylight, the plains lay clear. To the east purple was spreading into the sky, but west of me the trail to the lots was a lane of dusty gold light. I saw three crows pass over the willow thicket behind the barn and go cawing off into the blaze of western sky.

"Looks like the Lord would think it was trial enough, keeping me sixty-five years in this hell on earth," Grandma went on. "But I ain't the one to say."

11

"More than likely you ain't," Granddad said, looking up from his stick. "Scott, was you figurin' on getting into town tonight?"

"Thought I would," Hud said. "I didn't dress up to sit out here an' listen to Ma bitch."

"Now, Huddie," Granny said, changing her tune. "You just stay here tonight. There's a storm warning out from ten o'clock on."

"Fine," Hud said. "Maybe it'll rain an' green up this desert a little. If I sat around an' waited for ever little piss cloud to turn into a tornado, I never would go nowhere."

Granddad laid the stick on the steps and folded up his knife. "What time're you an' your mother plannin' to get off in the morning?" he asked.

Hud shrugged lazily. "Early enough," he said. "About four-thirty or five."

"I just wondered," Granddad said. "The doctors wanted Jewel to be in the hospital by dinnertime. If I was gonna make that long a drive I'd want all the sleep I could get."

"Hell," Hud said. "I ain't a hunnerd years old, like you. I don't need a week of sleep to be fresh."

Granddad didn't answer. The pickup rattled across the cattle guard to the south of the house, and Jesse waved at us as he drove on toward the barn.

"Say," Hud said. "Why don't you call the hide-and-rendering plant and have 'em come an' get that heifer. She just died this evenin'; she's still fresh enough to make soap." Hud and Lonzo had found the carcass on their way in that afternoon. Neither one of them knew what killed her, and Granddad hadn't gone out to take a look.

"Oh, I don't believe I will," Granddad said. "Fore I go to bed I'll call Newt Garrett and get him to come out and take a look at her in the morning. I'm kinda curious about what killed her. Lonzo's out there now keepin' off the buzzards."

"That's the stuff," Hud said, swelling up. "Call in some horse's ass to take your money. Don't never bother asking me what I think about anything."

"Well," Granddad said, "Newt ain't no what-you-say, and you ain't no authority on cattle diseases. I ain't either. This may be something I need to know about."

"Why, sure it will," Hud said, laughing his hard sharp laugh. "It'll be just bad enough he'll have you vaccinate ever head you own. And Newt's a vaccine salesman." He spit again, into the flower beds.

"That don't automatically make him dishonest," Granddad said, giving Hud a steady look. "You just concentrate on getting your mother to the hospital all in one piece, and I'll tend to my cattle."

"Sure, boss," Hud said, grinning down at Granddad. He swung himself off the rail and stood up, stretching his long arms above his head. Just then the dogs began to bark, and Jesse came around the corner of the house. The three of them hadn't quite got used to him, and they sniffed around his pants

13

legs. Jesse was dragging his game leg a little, looking dead tired.

"Why, hello, wild horse," Hud said. "Lose your crutch?"

Jesse gave him a tired, uneasy grin, and didn't try to say anything. Hud's style was strange to him, and around Hud he never knew quite what to say.

"You might get you a roller skate . . ." Hud started, but Granddad cut him off.

"Get 'em turned out all right?" he asked. "I hated to work you so late, but I didn't see no other way to do it."

Jesse took off his mashed-up straw hat and fingered the shaggy black hair on the back of his neck. "Why, yes," he said, "I got 'em unloaded all right." Actually, Hud exaggerated about Jesse's gimpy leg. As cowboys go, he was in good shape.

"Son, go in and get Halmea to scare Jesse up some supper," Granddad said. "He looks like he needs to graze a little."

"I could sure eat a bite," Jesse said. "I believe I'll go get me a drink of your well water to warm up on."

"Well, where's your manners?" Grandma snapped, her loud old voice surprising us all. "You ain't even got the politeness to say hello to me," she said. "I been sittin' here waitin'."

"Why, excuse me," Jesse said. "My goodness, I didn't even notice you, Miz Bannon."

"Go on an' get your drink," Granddad said. "It

don't make no difference." I could tell he was about to get out of snuff with her and her son. Jesse ducked his head toward her as politely as he could, and stepped back around the house.

"Good riddance," Grandma said. She had gone to fanning herself with an old Sunday-school fan she kept under the cushion of the rocker. "Help me back in the house, Lonnie," she said. "This night air's gettin' too cool."

"Let the boy alone, Jewel," Granddad said. "If you can't get in an' out under your own power just stay where you are awhile."

That made her fan a little faster. "I ought to know better than to ask a Bannon," she said. "Help me in, Huddie."

Hud laughed his quick, crow-caw laugh. "Hell, Momma, I can't," he said. "I'm just aworkin' from the shoulders down. If Homer Bannon says for you to get in by yourself, that's the way you better get in." His open-top Ford sat in front of the yard gate, and he stepped off the porch and strode lazily across the darkening yard. "Don't you folks lock the storm cellar," he said. "I may come aswimmin' in." He kicked one of the dogs back through the gate, shut it, and slipped under the wheel of his car. The Ford had a special horn, a cattle-caller, and Hud gave it a long scary blow as he gunned away. He kept the car in second for a mile or more, the rough, blasting sound of his mufflers loud in the evening stillness.

Grandma got up without saying a word and went into the house. In a minute there was a loud blast of static, and then the moany sound of a gospel song seeped out through the open screen door. Granddad looked like he'd just as soon be by himself, so I went around the house, meaning to see about Jesse's supper.

He was standing under the windmill, his Levis unbuttoned. He had taken his soaked shirttail out of his pants and was letting the cool night air dry the sweat on his stomach. We could still hear the fading sound of Hud's mufflers as he squealed onto the highway and off toward Thalia.

"He drives that thing, don't he?" Jesse said. "Is the old lady still pretty mad?"

"Not at you," I said.

He ran his fingers through his thick black hair. "I never could get along with old women," he said. "My own grandma give me hell as long as she lived. So did Ma. I had one aunt I could kinda be easy with, but I lost track a her."

"You ready to eat?" I asked him.

"Let me get my shirttail in," he said. "Your grandma might come in the kitchen and catch me." He quickly lowered his pants and smoothed down the wet tails of his heavy khaki shirt, then buttoned the Levis again. "Lord, I need a haircut," he said. "Been a month or more since I had one."

When we got in the kitchen, Halmea was back with *True Romances,* but the ice-cream freezer was gone from the sink, and the dishes had at least been stacked in the red dishpan. She laid the magazine down when she saw Jesse, but he just grinned at her. I snatched the magazine before she could pick it up again, and began to thumb through it myself.

"Weak readin'," I said. "How about gettin' Jesse some supper?"

"Just Mistah Jesse?" she said. "Nothin' fo' you?"

"Might set me a plate," I said. "I can eat a few beans."

She got up, grinning timidly at Jesse, and went to the cabinet. Jesse was someone Halmea hadn't felt out very well, and she walked easy when he was in the kitchen. I plopped down at the table and opened the magazine, while Jesse went down the hall to wash. Through the open door to the dining room I could hear Grandma's radio blaring—when she listened to preaching the whole household got a sermon. *"Keep on,"* the preacher said. *"Keep on adrinkin' your liquor, apitchin' your parties. . . ."* I got up and kicked the dining room door shut. Halmea was standing all spraddle-legged, reaching in the icebox for a jar of pickles, and I tried to give her the hip when I went by. But she straightened up too quick. "Go on," she said, "befo' you wets you didy." She had heard Granddad tell me that one time, and she thought I'd be real insulted to hear it from her. "Don't tear up my storybook," she said. "I ain't done with it yet."

Jesse came in then, his sleeves rolled up to the

elbow, his thin neck red from the scrubbing he had given it. He sat down across the table from me and began to fiddle with his fork, a little impatiently. Halmea put a platter of cold roast beef on the table first, then a bowl of red beans in thick, brownish gravy, a little plate of fresh-washed radishes and carrots, some plum-sized tomatoes, and a few sliced onions in a bowl of vinegar. Jesse took some of everything and went to eating, not waiting for his tea. I just dished out a few beans, and an onion slice or two.

"Light bread's all gone," Halmea said. "Kin you-all make out on carn bread tonight?"

"That'll hit the spot," Jesse said, looking up from his plate. "Could you spare me a glass of buttermilk to go with it?"

"Spare you a gallon of it," she said. She fished a slab of coarse yellow corn bread out of the oven and set it where we could help ourselves, then got the big pottery crock of buttermilk out of the icebox and poured us each a glassful.

"I believe I'll have a glass a dat myself," she said. "If you gentlemens don't mind."

Jesse had his mouth full, but he nodded for her to sit down, and she went to the cabinet to get a glass. He was almost through eating already, and I had barely finished a small plate of beans. He ate as if he expected someone to snatch his plate out from under him before he got enough.

"Where's old Lonzo?" he asked, wiping his

mouth. Before I could tell him, we all heard the loud moaning whistle of the train, coming across the plains from the south.

"He's out watching that carcass," I said. "Granddad wants the vet to look at it before it gets scattered."

Halmea had pulled up a chair, and was busy crumbling the cold yellow corn bread into her buttermilk. When she had enough crumbled up, she stirred it around with her spoon. "You-all hollah when you need somethin'," she said.

"I went by and seen Hank Hutch for a minute," Jesse said. He reached in his frayed shirt pocket for a package of cigarettes. "That feller's working himself to death."

Hank was our neighbor, a young cowboy about thirty years old who lived just across the highway. He worked for Granddad when there was a lot of work to do. When there wasn't, he cowboyed for other people, pumped a little oil lease the other side of Thalia, and picked up whatever work he could shoeing horses for the ranchers. He had a wife and three little girls, and was just barely keeping his head above water. He and I got along fine what little we were together.

Jesse wadded up his napkin and dropped it in his plate. "That's a hell of a way to live," he said. "I hate to see an old boy scratchin' at two or three jobs thataway, never knowin' nothin' but work and want. I believe I'd just as soon throw a life away as work it out like he's doing. Hard on him an' hard on his kids and womenfolk. Makes me glad I ain't married. Least there's one worry I ain't got."

Halmea snorted, her mouth half-full of corn bread and milk. A few drops of milk worked out of the corner of her mouth and trickled down her brown chin, but she wiped the stream away with her wrist.

"Dat's one worry you need," she said, giving him one of her slow, half-sassy looks. I saw she had gotten over being uneasy of Jesse in a hurry. I was so surprised by what she said I almost had to leave the table. She was always coming out with something strange in front of strangers. But I guess it embarrassed me more than it did Jesse, because he just drug on his cigarette and shook his head. He even gave her a tired grin. I saw them sit there looking at each other, beginning to get friendly, and in a way that made me feel alone and restless and left out. It's a way older people have: without even meaning to they let people younger than them know they aren't in the same club. Halmea leaned her elbows on the table and drank her buttermilk, halfway ready to laugh at me and Jesse both; there were beads of sweat on her face, and her heavy nigger breasts pouched out her gray dress. She chuckled to herself about something, a quick chuckle I always got a kick out of hearing. Jesse had tilted his chair back against the way, and was looking at Halmea through the smoke of his cigarette. There was something sad about Jesse, it was just on him, like his washed-out Levis and frazzled khakis. All the time I knew him, I never really saw him look comfortable. Something in him would need to brood, like something in Halmea would chuckle.

For a minute, nobody said a word. Then Halmea raised her glass to take a big swallow of buttermilk, and I saw the dark, sweaty wad of hair under her arm, and part of her stretched white brassière. While the two of them sat there looking so relaxed, I had to sip my buttermilk and squirm, thinking about Halmea. Once when I had the dogs up in the barn loft looking for rats, she had walked out in the weeds below me to a hen nest. I barely looked her way, but the minute I did she hiked her dress and squatted in the green broomweeds to pee. She went on gathering her eggs and never saw me, but I never did forget that glimpse, and if I happened to pass behind her while she was working at the sink, and saw one of her dark loose breasts when she raised her arm for something, it got to me worse than if all the girls in high school had shown up in the study hall naked.

Finally Jesse looked up and stamped out his cigarette. "I don't see it," he said. "A poor boy like me's got to be lucky to get along, just like it is, and if he's got a family he needs to be two or three times as lucky. So far I ain't even been lucky enough for myself."

Halmea was getting surer of Jesse by the minute, and when she got surer she just got more audacious.

21

"Sheew," she said, "don't tell me. A man by himself just like de fishline without de hook. He ain't gonna snag on nothin', dat away."

Jesse smiled, but he didn't laugh. He looked like he just didn't have the energy for more than a smile.

"Go on," Halmea said. "I knows about menfolks, or I ain't know anything."

Then we heard the tap of Granddad's boots as he came down the hall toward his bedroom. The sound of the radio had stopped, so Grandma had already gone to roost. Granddad stopped by the kitchen door and looked in at us, his coffee-can spittoon in one hand. "It's bedtime for us old folks," he said. "Jesse, that vet won't be here very early, I don't imagine. We don't need to get up till six or so."

"Okay," Jesse said, reaching under the chair for his hat. "If I'm awake I may get up and work that colt a little. I couldn't sleep late if you paid me to."

"Do what you want," Granddad said. "If the vet gets through in time we may try to fix a little fence. Good night." He started to go to his bedroom, then turned back. "You-all might keep an eye on the clouds," he said. "Jewel thinks it's goin' to storm."

When he had gone on and shut his bedroom door, Halmea got up and went quickly down the hall. I finished my buttermilk, and got up to walk Jesse to the bunkhouse. Halmea caught us about the back door and handed Jesse an armload of sheets and towels. "I fo'got dis mornin'," she said.

"Much obliged," Jesse said. "That bunkhouse gets pretty dusty. Enjoyed the supper."

"You welcome," she said. "Now you-all shoo." We were going anyway, but it was a good thing. Sooner or later every night Halmea would decide it was cleaning-up time, and when she did it was a good policy to stay out of her way. I had picked up her magazine as I went out, just to devil her, and before I got off the porch steps she hollered at me to bring it back. I took it back in and pitched it on the table, to tempt her. On the cover it had a picture of a bride crying into her veil, and under it it said MAMA, SET ME FREE.

"When you gonna be a bride, Halmea?" I said as I went out. I knew she had already been one a time or two, and I liked to tease her about it. I heard her deep bubbly chuckle after I slammed the door.

Jesse was waiting for me in the yard. He had just been on the ranch a week, but I was already in the habit of trailing him down to the bunkhouse every night. He stopped by the storm cellar to light a cigarette, and in the flicker of the match I saw his thin, hungry-looking face. The dogs were giving his pants legs another sniffing.

"Ain't that a fine old sycamore tree," he said, nodding toward it. The big tree stood just a few feet from the back door, and some of its longest limbs waved over the house. When I was at the Tarzan age I had practically lived in it.

"Lord I wish I had me a place with a few trees like that 'un on it," Jesse said regretfully. He

23

started down the thin foot trail toward the bunk-house, and I tagged along for the conversation. "It'd be an accomplishment," he said. I got around him and opened the bunkhouse door for him, then switched on the lights. He set the bedclothes down on an empty cot. The house was just one long bare room, with five or six steel cots in it, and a little partitioned-off lavatory and shower bath down at one end. There were a card table or two, a few chairs, and a couple of shaving mirrors on the wall. Lonzo and Jesse had taken about three mattresses apiece and piled them on their cots to make the sleeping a little softer. Their beds were rumpled, and the sheets on them gritty with the blown-in sand. What few clothes they had hung on the ten-penny nails that Granddad had driven into the wall years before. Neither Jesse nor Lonzo stayed in the bunkhouse any longer than they had to, and neither bothered to clean it up. Spider webs hung in the ceiling corners, and the floors were as gritty as the sheets.

Jesse sat down on his cot and began to pull off his tight-fitting dusty boots. "And you're just seven-teen," he said, surprising me.

"Not for long," I said. "My birthday's in September."

But I don't think Jesse was even thinking of me when he spoke. "My God," he said. "When I was seventeen I never got enough of anything." He set his boots carefully under the cot and began to unbutton his khaki shirt. "Summer I was that age, I

was workin' on a hayin' crew around Chillicothe,"
he said, looking regretful, like he would. "You'd
think pitchin' them big old bales of alfalfa up and
down all day woulda been enough exercise, but not
then it wasn't. I had an old boy named DeWayne
working on the same crew with me, and we bought
us a '27 Chevy and kept it tied together with bailin'
wire all that summer. We made ever square dance
and rodeo and honky-tonk in the country, and I
don't know which we run the hardest, that car or
the country girls that showed up at the dances." He
hung his dirty shirt over the back of the chair.
"Boy, boy," he said. "I do-ce-doed and chased
them girlish butts around many a circle that summer."

I could listen all night when Jesse got to going
back over his life, but the story never lasted long
enough, and it always ended with him getting
tireder and more sad. He sat on the edge of the cot,
stretching his lank, white stomach, and arching his
feet to get the boot-stiffness out of them.

"But, hell," he said. "You're big enough to get
out and do your own rarin' and tearin', without no
pattern a mine. Just so you get all the good you can
outa seventeen right now, because it sure wears out
in a hurry. Or did for me." Then he leaned back on
the cot, still wearing his Levis and socks. "What I
need is about eight hours on this squeaking cot.
Turn out that light for me, will you?"

I was in such a listening mood that I hated to
leave, but I could see Jesse was worn to a nub. I

went to the door, and switched off the light. "See you *mañana*," he said. "Lord, I'm tired."

I guess he had reason to be worn out, but when I went out the door I felt like I wouldn't ever need to sleep. What little Jesse had said about his running around just made me a little more restless than I usually was, and I was usually crazy with it. I wished I had something wild and exciting to do. But I didn't have an old wired-up Chevy, and it was too late to go anywhere in the pickup, and if I had taken it and gone there would just have been Thalia to go to, just an empty courthouse square to drive around. I went to the windmill, but instead of climbing up to the platform I got a drink and sat down in the thick cool yard grass, leaning my back against the wooden frame. I thought about the three nights I had got to spend in Fort Worth, the summer before. Granddad had gone down to buy some cattle, and at night he sat in the lobby of the big hotel, talking to another old cowman, and let me do pretty much as I pleased. He thought I was going to picture shows, I guess, but instead I wandered up and down Main Street, that one long street, under the city lights. I went way down to the south end of the street, to where they have the gospel missions and the Mexican picture shows, where the wild-looking people were as thick as crickets under the yellow neon. Pretty soon I discovered that I could slip in the hillbilly bars, into one of the dark booths, and get them to serve me all the beer I wanted. I sat there gripping the cold sweaty bottles and listening to the laughter, the shuffling dancers, the sad hillbilly music. But what I got in Fort Worth was just a taste, just a few mouthfuls of excitement; and leaning against the windmill, I couldn't think of anything I wanted more than to go back for another swallow or two.

In a few minutes the back door slammed, and Halmea came across the dark yard, on her way to her little house for the night. She was looking down, and didn't notice me, so when she got almost to the gate I gave a loud hiss, like a bull snake makes. She jumped and dropped her magazine, then stood there scared to death, twisting her neck around. She saw me then, but she still wasn't sure about the snake.

"Deys a snake in dis yard," she said, not making a move. "I stay right here an' watch him, and you see can you slip aroun' easy and get the flashlight an' de hoe." I guess she actually thought she had the snake spotted; she never took her eyes off the ground.

I flopped back in the grass and hissed again, laughing before I finished the hiss. "I might know," she said. In a few minutes she'd be boiling, but right then she was so relieved she just snatched the magazine and went on out the gate.

"Ou-la, Halmea," I said. I knew she wouldn't get snake off her mind for days. I could just see her, tiptoeing down the path, taking about half an hour to make it to her house. Every time she stopped she'd hear an old bull rattler sliding through the grass. And if she didn't find him in the grass, she'd look him up in her horoscope.

When Halmea was out of hearing, I lay back in the long, uncut Bermuda, and wondered about what all Jesse had said. It still made me itch to be off somewhere, with a crowd of laughers and courters and beer drinkers, to go somewhere past Thalia and Wichita and the oil towns and Sno-Cone stands, into country I'd never seen. I was glad Jesse had come: he could open things up. Granddad didn't talk to me much any more, and anyway, Granddad and I were in such separate times and separate places. I had got where I would rather go to Thalia and goof around on the square than listen to his old-timy stories.

In a little while the sand ants began to sting my wrists, and I got up. I went around behind the smokehouse to piss. In my gradeschool days we had hung carcasses in the smokehouse, beeves and hogs that Granddad and the cowboys butchered on frosty mornings in November. For a while then there would be cracklin's, and salty smells, and the dogs would be fighting over the pigs' feet. But now the beeves and hogs were in the locker plant in Thalia, and the smokehouse only held broken lawn mowers and spades and pieces of harness. I heard a dog yapping, stranded somewhere out in coyote country. As I went in the house I noticed the lightning flickering off to the southwest, and saw that the stars were blotted out in that direction. But in June in our part of the country, clouds and lightning were no novelty, and I didn't pay them any attention.

When I got upstairs I didn't feel very sleepy, so I got out *From Here to Eternity* and read over some of the scenes with Prew and Maggio in the New Congress Hotel. I thought it was about the best book ever to come to our drugstore newsstand, and I kept reading some of the chapters in it over and over. Those parts about the dances in the New Congress reminded me a lot of my nights in Fort Worth; the people in the book seemed a lot like the ones I saw. Then I read the part where the sergeant got her the first time, and put the book back in my suitcase in the closet. I turned off the light and stretched on top of the covers to sleep, smelling the green dewy ranchland through the screen.

CHAPTER

2

1.

Hud didn't have to run from any tornado, but he must have got in some kind of a storm because he didn't come in till six-thirty the next morning. Jesse and I were eating breakfast when we heard the convertible slide up to the back gate. Grandma had been up and ready to go to Temple for two or three hours, and she run into the kitchen to give him an eating out; but Hud looked so red-eyed and wild she just went on back to her room and began to gather up her hatboxes. I finished my breakfast and went down to the barn and drove Granddad's Lincoln to the house so we could load it. Granny had packed enough stuff for an arctic expedition.

Jesse and me were admiring the car when she came tapping out the back door, all powdered and painted, wearing a big green hat with a veil on it. She might have been going to the fair she was in such a good humor. Granddad brought out the first load of suitcases, and Jesse and I hurried in and got the rest.

"Well, I'm ready," Grandma said. "Where's Huddie? I don't intend to wait no longer. If I got to go be cut up I'm ready right now." Granddad helped her into the car, and stood by the door to try and keep her from jumping out again for some foolishness. Hud came out in about five minutes, fresh-looking enough to have slept for a week. He pitched his canvas army bag in the back seat, and got under the wheel.

"Now be careful, Scott," Granddad said, one hand still on the car door. "If you get tired, why, stop and sleep." He took out his checkbook and fountain pen, and used the hood of the Lincoln for a desk as he wrote out the check. He folded it carefully and handed it across the car seat to Hud.

"That ought to take care of the hotel and such," he said. Hud already had the motor running, and for a minute I wished it were me who was driving away. Granddad patted Grandma on the shoulder. "Jewel, you get on back here as soon as you can," he said. "We're liable to need you."

Grandma was looking straight ahead, impatient to be off. Her eyes were snappy as a bird's, and she wanted no conversation. "Don't be ahurryin' me home," she said. "You just tend to your ranch. I'm gonna take my time with this operation."

"We're gone," Hud said, throwing the car in gear.

"Watch out for the kids and the cripples, and don't buy no vaccine factory." The wheels spun a minute in the thin gravel of the road, and the car jerked away.

Jesse said he had to go where he could get the leverage on his bowels, and Granddad told me to start loading a few posts in the pickup, so we could fence a little when we got the veterinary business done. I backed the old white pickup up to the post pile, and had loaded about ten or twelve of the smallest cedars I could find when I saw Newt Garrett drive up to the house in his muddy blue De Soto. Granddad was still in the house, so I left the posts to go tell him Newt had come. About the time I got to the back porch, Granddad came out.

Old Newt was still sitting in his car, with the motor still running. He hated to walk worse than any man in the country, and wouldn't unless he absolutely had to. He was an old-timer, nearly as old as Granddad. Once he had been a Texas Ranger, and he had enough pension to keep him alive, and enough oil money on top of it to make him about half-rich. He spent most of his time playing moon in the Thalia domino hall, but he still did a little horse-doctoring for the people he liked. He had lost his voice box in a cancer operation, and had to talk by pressing an electric buzzer against his throat. For the last few years he had been so contrary that nobody but Granddad would have anything to do with him, and Granddad just called him in once in a while when some heifer was having a hard time squeezing out her first calf. Granddad shook hands with him through the window of the car.

"Get any rain?" he asked. That was always the first question.

Newt took out his buzzer and stuck it to his throat. "Sprinkle," he said. "Late last night. Nuff to wash the dust off my chickens." Newt was a funny old fart anyway, and the dry way he buzzed out his words tickled me to death.

"Kill your motor and get out," Granddad said. "We'll go in my pickup. I don't believe we could get across them roads in that car."

Jesse came up about that time, and when Newt finally got out, Granddad introduced him. Newt shook his hand, and then pointed at the De Soto.

"Ain't no automobile," he said. "See. It's a slide. It ain't no higher than a slide." He got his bag of instruments out of the back seat and started for the barn.

Jesse and I tagged them down the trail and got in the back of the pickup, on my twelve little cedars. Just as Granddad was about to drive off he remembered Lonzo, out there without any breakfast, and he drove back up to the house and sent me in to fix a plate.

The minute Grandma left the house Halmea must have unplugged the living room radio and carried it to the kitchen. When I came in the back door, it was on the cabinet, blaring rock 'n' roll, and Halmea was putting on a dance all by herself.

"Listen at it," she said, slapping her hands together and slide-stepping in front of the sink. The song was "Honeylove," and the loud honky saxophone practically curled the wallpaper. If Granddad hadn't been a shade deaf he would have heard it from the pickup. But old juicy Halmea just grinned and snapped her fingers at me and went on dancing. Then she got tickled at me or at herself or something and giggled till she could barely keep from falling over. Finally the song stopped, but even then she kept on shuffling a little to a tune of her own.

"Cut it off," I said. "Fix me a plate for Lonzo right quick. Granddad's waitin'."

She already had a plate in her hands, and was crossing to the icebox. "Dat Mistah Bannon," she said. "Dat man hurry himself too much. He ain't got no slowdown to him, whut's de trouble."

"He's made it eighty-two years without relaxing," I said. "Couldn't you get any hillbilly this morning?"

"I ain't dancin' no hillbilly," she said, piling cold roast and sausage and boiled eggs on the plate. "I'm just *dancin'* dancin', dis mornin'." When she had a good pile, she covered the plate with aluminum foil and set it on the cabinet for me. I started for the door, but she stopped me. "Mistah Lonzo needs some coffee," she said. The radio had started up a

Fats Domino song, and she was slow-dancing across the room with the percolator.

"If you drop that coffee your ass is mud," I said. Then I almost dropped it myself, corking the Thermos. When I went out the screen door I could hear her bare feet slapping the linoleum as she went on with her lonesome, happy dance.

Newt was sitting with his voice box in his hand, so I knew Granddad had been getting a lot of dry conversation. I handed Newt the lunch to hold, and climbed in the back. Jesse sat with his back against the cab, smoking a cigarette and looking glum. I told him about Halmea cutting up, but it didn't make much impression on him. "Some girl," he said. Watching him, as Granddad crept along down the feed road, I thought what a strange man Jesse was. In no time he could turn so gloomy and sad it made you uncomfortable to be around him. He looked out across the pastures with a disappointed expression on his face. When we came to the gate leading into the west pasture I jumped out to open it, but it was a hard gate, and he had to come and help me hook it shut.

We had to go about four or five miles across the big pasture to get to where the heifer was. I sat back against the endgate, enjoying the clear blue sweep of sky, and the early, grassy smell of the range. Finally Granddad stopped the pickup on top of a little ridge, and we got out. Newt looked kinda contrary. He was so famous for his laziness that I wondered how far Granddad could get him to walk, especially across the wet pastures. It was later than it should have been, and getting hot.

"She's over this way a little piece," Granddad said. "I better not try and drive any farther. Can you walk it?"

"Oh yes, oh yes," Newt buzzed. "Go ahead." Jesse and I followed them, not feeling very useful.

"We might as well astayed an' fenced," Jesse said. "I don't know what help we'll be here."

We waded through a patch or two of high prairie weeds, getting our Levis damp almost to the knees. It had come the heaviest dew I'd nearly ever seen. We topped a little rise and saw Lonzo sitting under a big mesquite tree about fifty yards away. He was asleep, a twenty-two rifle laying across his lap. The carcass of the heifer lay about twenty or thirty yards to the south of him, and there must have been fifty buzzards sitting in the trees around it. As we came in sight one of the buzzards flopped to the ground, and began a slow, cautious waddle toward the heifer. The others stayed in the trees, nodding their scabby bald heads now and then, and raising their wings.

Lonzo woke up when he heard us coming, and he tried to pretend he had just been possuming, to get the buzzards to come down. He began to shoot, working the little pump-action gun as fast as he could, six or eight shots before he ran out of bullets. Most of the shots kicked up grass stems and little puffs of dirt on one side of the bird or the other, but at least one shot hit him and knocked a wad of tar-colored feathers from his back. He took off anyway, rose gradually, turned and flew right over us, not more than fifteen feet high. I could almost have jumped up and grabbed his scaly feet. All the other buzzards rose too, taking off from the limbs like spring-board divers; only they sprung upward into the air, and swirled up to where they looked like flies against the blue pane of sky.

Lonzo stood up and began to reload his twenty-two. He was a tall, lank, gangly boy from Oklahoma who had been working for Granddad nearly two years. He claimed the only thing he'd ever got enough of his whole life was work, and that when it came to food or pussy or beer he always came out on the short end. He was easily satisfied, though, and if he couldn't get any of those other things, he would settle for lots of sleep.

"Look at them cowardly sonsabitches," he said, waving the gun at the buzzards. Newt stepped behind Granddad when he did that. He thought Lonzo was crazy and dangerous.

"Would you look at them chickenshits," Lonzo went on, his Adam's apple jerking in his thin neck. "You couldn't keep 'em scared off with artillery." It surprised some people that Granddad kept Lonzo on, because he didn't know beans about cowboying, and didn't show much talent for learning. Hud said right off that Lonzo only knew how to talk and eat and fuck and fist-fight and chop cotton, and that the only thing he was a top hand at was eating. "See there," he said, pointing to where three buzzards lay dead on the ground. "Pretty good shootin' for a twenty-two. I'll get some more if they ever settle down."

"Easy now," Jesse said. "Leave a few to keep the country clean."

I handed Lonzo his plate and Thermos, and he started over to his bedroll to eat, but Newt stopped him. Newt had been eying the dead buzzards, and he got his talk-piece out.

"Broke the law," he said. He really thought he was putting Lonzo in his place. "Big fine for killing buzzards."

Lonzo had picked a hard-fried egg off the plate and was gobbling it down, the twenty-two dangling carelessly from the crook of his arm. He had his mouth full when Newt buzzed, and he took his time answering.

"No shit?" he said finally. He got a kick out of Newt. "Is there really a law like that?"

"Oh yes," Newt buzzed. "Oh yes."

Lonzo squatted on his heels and chewed another egg. "Well," he said, "I was raised in Oklahoma. Up there they don't have as many foolish laws as they do other places." He looked up and grinned at Newt. "I had an old boy tell me once, he was a highway patrolman, that the law was meant to be interpurted in a leenent manner. That's what I try to do, myself. Sometimes I lean to one side of it, sometimes I lean to the other." He laughed at himself, or at Newt, and uncorked the Thermos of coffee. Newt acted insulted and went over to the carcass, where Granddad was. Lonzo poured hot coffee into the Thermos cup, the smoke rising from the glass rim of the bottle. He winked and blew on the coffee to cool it. "Looks to me like them boys in Austin oughta have something better to do than make laws about a lot of goddamn buzzards. Don't it look that way to you?" He took the three last pieces of sausage in his hand and slung the paper plate over his shoulder into the mesquite. Then he ate the sausages in about three bites. "I had to hump to keep them bastards off," he said. "I finally propped my flashlight so it shone right on the heifer, an' whenever one stepped into the light, I let him have it." He stood up, picking his teeth with his thumbnail.

We went over, then, and watched old Newt poke around on the heifer. For about five minutes he didn't do anything but squat in front of her head and look at her, working his lips like he was making conversation. Granddad squatted down beside him. He had taken out his pocketknife and was whittling on the dry stem of a ragweed, shaving off the thin brittle bark. The lines in his face were deep, that morning, like ruts in road, his whiskers snow white against his brown face. He looked at the heifer curiously, but he didn't seem too disturbed.

He had lost a lot of cattle at one time or another in his life, and one dead heifer didn't discourage him much.

The heifer was laying on her side, her two top legs sticking out in the air. She was swelled up with bloat, but there was no smell to amount to anything. Hud said she had just died when he found her. She wasn't cut, or crippled-looking, and there was no swelling on her that could have meant a snakebite.

Finally Newt stood up and fiddled for his buzzer. "I don't know," he said. "I don't know. Beats me. We might look in her stomach."

"Now's when we all need clothespins," Jesse said, rolling up his shirtsleeves. We moved the heifer like Newt wanted her, and he took a long knife and opened her up. There was stink enough then, but so far as we could tell, it was just work wasted. "Beats me," Newt buzzed. His old, burnt, freckledly face looked solemn. He left the heifer and walked over to the good shade tree where Lonzo had his bedroll. The rest of us followed him over.

"Homer," Newt buzzed. "Homer. Get on the telephone, call up the state vet. He might know."

That surprised us all, but it like to floored Granddad. It was the first time anybody had heard Newt Garrett recommend another veterinary; and a state vet on top of that.

"Why, what in the world?" Granddad said. "Is it

all that complicated? I never have much doings with them fellers if I can help it."

Newt didn't back up a step. "Better call," he said. "Might be something serious. I don't know. I can't tell. Homer, better call."

"I never figured on havin' to call in the government," Granddad said. "I ain't sure I want to, just for one heifer." Granddad had got so he would walk a mile rather than involve himself with the government offices, and even so, compared to Hud he thought they were little darlings. Hud plain hated the mention of government. One of the worst things between Hud and Granddad was that Granddad had let him go in the service when he could have kept him out.

"Play safe," Newt buzzed. "They may all get sick if you don't."

"What makes you think so?" Granddad said.

But old Newt had his private stubborn streak, and he wouldn't volunteer a word. Granddad hummed and hawed with him a little longer, then Newt got mad and stuck his buzzer in his pocket and headed for the pickup. Granddad waved for Jesse and Lonzo to come over.

"He wants to get to the domino hall," he said. "Jesse, I guess you better stay out here awhile. I'll take Lonzo in with me and let him snooze a little. Come on to the pickup and get the water can, so you won't parch."

Jesse went with us to the pickup, and carried the

gray metal can back through the weeds. As we were driving away we heard the quick pop of the twenty-two. It was hot in the back of the pickup, and Granddad was just poking along, driving as slow as he could and stay in high gear. Lonzo didn't care. He took off his hat and let the wind dry his sweaty head. "I got the best end of the deal after all," he said. "He ain't gonna kill no buzzards in the daytime. Them cowardly bastards are too smart."

2.

After dinner Halmea filled some empty ice-cream cartons with beans and meat and tea, and I put them in an empty vaccine crate and carried them out to Jesse ahorseback. Some of the tea sloshed out, but I got there with most of what I started with. I was hoping Jesse would be in a talking mood, so I could stay awhile; but it turned out just the opposite. He looked hot and down-in-the-mouth, and acted like he didn't much want me around. I left him right away, and rode home across the still, weedy pastures, wondering how to spend the afternoon.

When I got to the lots I loped out to the big tank that stood about half a mile north of the barn. I wanted to water my horse, and check on the bullfrog crop. It was a big, deep tank, with a gravel bottom. There was a nice stand of cottonwoods, and the bank had a good covering of Bermuda grass. Halmea and her colored friends loved to fish in it. There were some nice catfish in it, and a lot of croppie, but about all I ever caught were the little five-inch perch. My life's ambition was to get Halmea to go in swimming with me some time, but so far she wouldn't even wade.

I unsaddled, and decided to give it another try. She was in the living room, flopped on the satin-covered divan that was Grandma's pride and joy. She was laying on her stomach, humming and filing her fingernails.

"Let's go swimmin'," I said. "The tank's like bath water."

"I ain't no paddler," she said, barely looking up. She had kicked her red sandals off, and they lay on the living room rug, about ten yards apart.

"You could be," I said. "With feet like yours."

"Sheew, my feet's just barely do to walk on. We might go fishin' though."

"Too much trouble," I said. "I'd have to scrounge up bait."

Then she sat up, pushing her heavy, kinked black hair off her forehead, tucking some behind her ears. "Let's do go fishin'," she said. "I been in dis house too long. We got some liver fo' bait."

I hadn't thought of the liver, but I knew I wasn't going to sit around pulling out those worthless perch all afternoon, when all I really wanted was to see Halmea in the water. At least I wanted a chance to duck her a time or two.

"It's too windy to fish," I said. "Don't be so scared of the water."

She looked surprised, and then she gave me the slow grin. She had on a loose floppy dress, and her breasts rolled against it like cantaloupes when she sat up. "Sheew," she said, grinning. "Me scared a watah?" Then she fell back suddenly on the satin couch and haw-hawed, the deep careless laughter coming clear up from her guts it sounded like. "I got yo' number," she said.

"You got my nothin'," I said. "I just thought you might like to swim awhile, you look so bored."

"Who you foolin'?" she said. "Honey, it ain't Halmea." She laughed as if the funniest thing possible had just occurred to her. It was the laughing fit of her life, I guess, and she had to wipe the tears out of her eyes and off her cheeks. "Sugah, you plain as day," she said. "You don' want no fishin'." And she picked a copy of *Life* magazine off the floor and began to look through it, still laughing her rich, teasing laugh. I couldn't even get her interested in fishing, after that. "Go on, Mistah Tightpants," she said, giggling.

Finally I gave it up and went outside. Granddad had been after me for a week to cut the goat-heads in the chicken yard, so I sharpened my shovel and went at it. I worked like a demon, and in thirty minutes or so I had cut about ten thousand and only had a million or two to go. Halmea came out of the house, on the way to her little shack. She leaned on the chicken-yard fence a minute, grinning, the wind blowing her floppy dress against her legs.

"Can't you find no bait?" she said. She laughed and went on down the trail, and I got after the goat-heads, the sweat running down my face and into my eyes.

3.

Granddad had gone to Thalia, to see about the vet. When he came back he was silent and blue, and in spite of all we could say he went out and stood a turn watching the heifer. "You drive," he said to me, after supper. "I'm going out an' spell Jesse awhile." So I drove the pickup through the late, dusky pastures, and he looked out of the window at the bunches of cattle as we passed them. He didn't say two words. The sun had about thirty minutes to go when I parked the pickup on the ridge and we got out. That time of day the prairie smelled rich to me, stingy and sappy and green.

Jesse was stretched out on Lonzo's bedroll, resting. The buzzards were in some low mesquite trees, two or three hundred yards away.

"Why, I can stay out here tonight," Jesse said, surprised to see us.

"No, you go in an' eat an' rest awhile," Granddad said. He walked over and looked solemnly

45

down at the heifer. The green flies were buzzing and crawling in the open gut. Granddad had on a Levi jacket against the night cool, and his mashed-up brown Stetson was pulled down over his forehead. "The other vet's comin' in the morning," he said. "Maybe we'll be done with this before much longer."

Jesse and I went on back to the pickup, and I drove us home across the darkening pastures. Jesse was in a better humor than he had been that afternoon, and I hit him up to go to the picture show. He was agreeable, so while he ate cold supper for the second night in a row I went to the bunk-house and routed Lonzo out. He had flopped down asleep the minute he got through the door, without even taking off his Levis or his heavy khaki shirt, and of course he was lathered in his own sweat. I got him awake enough to convince him he wanted to go with us, and he dripped a little shower water on his head and put on some fresh clothes. He was still drugged and gloopy, and didn't say a word. We went out and set on the fender of the pickup, where it was cooler, and in a minute Jesse came out of the house and stopped to light his after-supper cigarette.

We got in, and I drove down the dark dirt road to the highway, swung on, and gigged the old pickup for all it was worth toward the lights of Thalia. Lonzo sat next to me, still half-asleep. One minute the town lights would be just ahead of us, bright against the dark sky, and the next minute we'd hit a little dip and they would fall out of sight. There was just the lights and the highway and off to the west a few stars overhead.

"Lonesome old night," Jesse said. I glanced over at him, and the tired lines of his face were softened and hidden by the dim light from the dashboard. A big lonesomeness hung over Jesse all right. "Better slow down," he said. "You'll run plumb through town before you can stop."

But I roared on into Thalia, fifty miles an hour right up to the square. I slowed down a little and circled it, parked in front of the lightbulbs and cardboard posters of the picture show. The pickup rolled against the curb hard enough to shake Lonzo out of his drunken stupor, and we got out and went in. When I was a kid in grade school Thalia had had two picture shows, but in those days the oil-field activity was big, and Thalia was a wild, wet sort of half boom town. Pretty soon the oil production fell off and the oil people took their cars and their dirty scrappy kids down the road to another field. The people who stayed voted to close the beer joints then, and after that there wasn't any place to go at night except the picture shows and the all-night trucker's café. A year or two later one of the shows closed up and they started using the billboards to run advertising for the one that hung on. That night there was an old picture playing, *Streets of Laredo*, with Gene Autry and Smiley Burnette. We all got popcorn and sat down to watch the previews. By the time the main show came on, Lonzo was wide awake and full of sass.

"Look at that silver mounted saddle," he said, snickering. "You couldn't lift that bastard on a horse with a goddamn crane."

"I met Gene Autry once," Jesse whispered. "Two years ago at the rodeo in Houston. Seemed like a strange man."

I don't know how he would be at the rodeo, but in the picture he was his chubby fat self, knocking the bad guys over like dominoes. Between Lonzo's snickering, and the little kids chasing themselves up and down the aisle, I could barely hear the picture. When *Streets of Laredo* was over they had one of those silly comedies where you were supposed to sing along with the bouncing golf ball. Lonzo wanted to sing with it, but he couldn't read fast enough to keep up with the ball, and everybody in the show got to laughing at him. I poked him in the ribs to make him quit, but he clipped me under the chin with his elbow, not noticing, and I had to sit and hold my breath for a minute, till my teeth stopped rattling. I kept forgetting how strong Lonzo was. Finally there was a newsreel showing the New York Yankees trotting across a baseball field in Florida, and it was time for the previews to start around again.

We left the show and drove down to the drive-in

so I could get a hamburger. Lonzo had missed his supper, so he got three. I offered to buy Jesse a root beer or something, but he just sat and smoked. I went up and put a quarter in the outdoor jukebox, played "Folsom Prison Blues" and "I'm in the Jail-house Now," and we all sat and listened while the hamburgers cooked.

"What do kids do for fun around here?" Jesse asked, watching the carhop hurrying around between the cars. She was making up to a carload of roughnecks, fixing to go out on the night's tower.

"Whatever there is," I said.

"What the hell is there?" Lonzo said. "About a dime's worth is all I can see."

Actually we didn't do an awful lot. There was the pool hall, the snooker and eight-ball tables. But most of the time we just rode around and talked, or hunted up girls to court. Once in a while we drove to the county line and bought some beer.

"I guess kids out here have to make their own," Jesse said. "It ain't that way in the cities, what I've seen."

"Lonnie oughta go to Oklahoma," Lonzo said. "Hell, we had some big times up there when I was growing up. All the girls put out."

"Put you out, you mean," Jesse said. He flipped his cigarette out the window. "But I guess this ain't so bad. Many a one grew up with less."

"Hell, they grew up in the wrong state if

they did," Lonzo said. "They oughta tried Oklahoma."

I saw some of my buddies over in another car, and I wished for a minute that I had left Lonzo and Jesse at home. If I had been by myself I might have got with the other boys and scared up something. I figured I'd try it the next chance I got. We got the hamburgers, and all the songs played, so we drove on back to the ranch. We flipped to see who would go out and replace Granddad, and Lonzo lost. He drove off, and Jesse and I stood a minute at the yard gate.

"Enjoyed the picture," he said, "but say, listen. When you get to wantin' to go make whoopee on your own, just say so and me and Lonzo'll catch up on our sleep. I don't like to see nobody in a cramp." He was quiet a minute, and then he went on. "I remember when I was about nineteen," he said. "I had been on my own, and I had to go back and start helpin' Dad. We had a cotton patch in Throckmorton County, right next to the highway that run in to Fort Worth an' Dallas and no tellin' where-all. I spent all my time following a couple a work mules around that field, and all day long folks would whiz by in their cars, going places I wanted to go. Don't think I wouldn't a given that whole run-down piece a land to a jumped in one a them cars and gone whizzing by some other pore bastard that had to work. I never could stand to be cramped up after that. I hate to see anybody in a cramp." He patted me on the shoulder, and strolled off through the darkness to the bunkhouse. I felt tired out. I went to my room and flipped through an old magazine or two, but when I saw the lights of Granddad's pickup coming along the prairie road, I pitched the magazines down and went to sleep.

CHAPTER

——————— 3 ———————

1.

I heard Granddad's steps on the stairs outside my door as I turned over. He came in and laid his hand on my shoulder. "Lonnie boy," he said. "Breakfast time." Then he went out of the gray room, and I knew that getting up was my responsibility. It looked misty outside, and I lay on a minute, my face nuzzled into the cool pillow. Then I heard the faraway slam of the screen door as Halmea came in to cook breakfast, and in a minute I heard "Let the Lower Lights Be Burning," the early theme song, coming from the kitchen radio. Jesse and Granddad were talking, standing on the porch just below me. When I heard them I swung my feet to the bare piny smoothness of the floor.

The light in the yard was timid yet, but I could see the heavy glisten of dew on the Bermuda grass, and smell the dampness of the gray range in the early breeze. While I was buttoning my stiff clean khaki shirt I heard the raspy voice of the radio announcer, bringing the five o'clock news. I put on my socks and went downstairs to the bathroom, my boots in my hand. I didn't feel woke up at all, and I remembered one bad morning when I had come downstairs with my eyes half-shut and got into the kitchen closet by mistake and pissed sleepily on the brooms.

When I came into the kitchen Halmea was standing by the stove, flipping grease over the eggs she was frying. She had on a clean blue dress, and looked too cheerful to fool with.

"Wish I could sleep till dinnah like you does," she said.

"Fry your eggs," I said, dragging a package of Post Toasties from the cabinet. Granddad and Jesse were already sitting at the table, eating eggs and bacon and sipping coffee from their saucers. I missed Lonzo, and remembered he was out on the range again. I poured milk over my Post Toasties, and began to read the advertising bullshit on the back of the box. I had read it a hundred times, but there was nothing else handy. By the time I got to biscuits and syrup Granddad and Jesse had carried their plates to the sink and gone out, and I had to sop up my sorghum in a hurry and follow them.

When I stepped off the back porch the sun was just coming up, striking all kinds of colors against the low mossy clouds that still hung in the west. My regular job was to scatter hay for the horses, so while Granddad and Jesse milked I climbed up in the high loft and kicked down a few dusty bales. By the time I had them in the racks the two full milk buckets were waiting to be carried to the house and strained. The milk was hot, and the foam on top fizzed a little as I lugged the buckets to the back porch. Halmea came out and helped me fix the cheesecloth on the blue milk strainer, and I slowly poured the two bucketfuls through. When I got back to the lots Granddad and Jesse were at the big water trough, trying to unstop a faucet. I went over, but I was just in the way.

"I believe here comes our man," Jesse said, looking up. A black Chevrolet was bumping down the rough road toward the barn; there were two men in the front seat.

The driver stopped the car beside the water trough, and the man riding got out. He was a short man, not as tall as I was, and he had a medical badge of some kind pinned on the front of his gabardine jacket. He came toward us holding out his hand, and looked friendly as could be.

"I'm Jimmy Burris," he said. "Good morning to you men. Looks like you-all need a plumber, not a vet."

"Oh, just a faucet clogged," Granddad said. The vet shook hands with all three of us; he nodded for his driver to get out, but the man sat behind the wheel and made like he hadn't noticed the nod. We all stood around a little stiff for a minute, everybody trying to think of what to say next. I wondered why the man in the car was so unsociable.

"Well," Granddad said finally. "I guess there's no use in us standing here till dinner. I imagine you've got other things to do today, and I know good and well I have. Let's go look at that carcass."

"Do we go in my vehicle or yours?" Mr. Burris asked.

"Let's go in mine," Granddad said. The vet waved for his driver to kill the motor, and the man got out. He was a big surly-looking man named Thompson; he just nodded when Mr. Burris introduced us. The vet got his bag, and we left.

For some reason, Jesse got in the pickup cab with Granddad and Mr. Burris, leaving me in the rear with Thompson. He chewed on a match, and didn't say anything. His face was red, and full of little chicken-track blood vessels, and his eyes didn't seem to quite match. When we got to the hard gate I was hoping he'd get out and get it, but he didn't make a move. I got it open all right, but I had a terrible wrestle shutting it. I was afraid somebody would have to come and help me, and keep me in the doghouse all morning. I managed, but I skinned up one hand good and proper.

"By god, you did get it," Thompson said. "I thought you was gonna have to leave it open. Didn't you have no Wheaties this morning?" I didn't say a word to him.

When we got to the heifer that morning, there was no time wasted. Lonzo was mad because we hadn't brought him breakfast, but there wasn't anything we could do about it. Granddad walked over and stood looking down at the heifer, and the veterinary followed him.

"There she is," Granddad said. The heifer smelled pretty bad, and the green flies were getting what the buzzards couldn't. Mr. Burris squatted by the heifer's head, looking at her shrunken jaws. He pursed his lips.

"Who cut this carcass open?" he said.

"Newt Garrett," Granddad said. "Was that the wrong thing to do?"

Mr. Burris didn't look up. "It could have been the very worst thing possible," he said. "I'll have to see." He put on some rubber gloves and got a knife out of his bag. While we stood watching him, careful not to get in his light, he cut out the heifer's tongue and put it in a bottle he had in his bag. He didn't look nearly as cheerful as he had when he stepped out of his car that morning.

"I wouldn't have believed this if I hadn't seen it," he said. "I'm not sure I believe it anyway. But we'll see." He stood up then, and faced Granddad. "Mr. Bannon, I'm afraid you may have something bad."

"I was kinda afraid of that myself," Granddad said. "Reason I had you look. I couldn't figure a heifer just dropping dead like that. Do you know for sure what it is?"

"Well, yes and no," the vet said. "Here, we might as well get away from this stink. I've got all I need. Let's go to the shade and talk cool. I'd like to find out a few things if you've got time."

"I've always had more of that than anything else," Granddad said. He didn't seem half as worried as Mr. Burris. He walked over to the big tree and squatted on his heels by Lonzo's bedroll. While Mr. Burris was taking off his rubber gloves, Granddad found him a little stick and began to whittle. He always did that, if he was still for two minutes. Squatting there with his brown hat pulled way down over his forehead he looked awful small and old, but awful determined. We went over and squatted too. Lonzo lay down on his quilt. Thompson stood with his arms folded, just in the edge of the shade. He acted like none of it was the least concern of his.

"Mr. Bannon," the vet said. "Have you by any chance bought any Mexican cattle in the last year or two? If this is the disease I think it is, it very seldom comes this far north."

Granddad looked up, not especially surprised. "It's been almost three years ago," he said. "I bought two hundred head of cows from a ranch down near Laredo. But I don't believe that heifer yonder was out of one of those cows."

"Oh, that wouldn't make any difference," Mr. Burris said. "I was just trying to line up some possibilities in my mind. I was hoping maybe we

57

could trace this thing down, but if it's been that long ago I don't guess it's worth the trouble." He was tapping one fist against his knee. "Mr. Bannon," he said, "how long would it take you to get your cattle together?"

"My cattle?" Granddad asked, surprised. "You mean the ones in this pasture, or all the ones I own? I could have this pasture here by sometime after dinner."

"No, I think we ought to at least look at them all," Mr. Burris said. "We're going to have to make an inspection, and the sooner the better."

"For what?" Granddad said. "Inspection for what?"

Mr. Burris was picking at a little scab on the back of his hand. "For what killed that heifer," he said. "Mr. Bannon, I hope I'm wrong, but I'm very much afraid you've got the worst kind of trouble a cattleman can have. I think that heifer died of hoof-and-mouth disease. Now my opinion isn't the final verdict, but just from the looks of things I think we better get to investigating this situation."

"Oh me," Granddad said. He kept his eyes on the stick. "I never thought it would be nothing like that."

For a minute nobody said anything. I was thinking of Hud, of how wild he would be when he got wind of it. Hud had done everything he could to keep Granddad from buying the Laredo cattle—he hated the whole South Texas area, and especially the Mexicans that were in it. He had picked out a bunch of cows in Colorado that he claimed were a whole lot better than the ones Granddad bought, and he never let Granddad forget it.

"I wish you'd tell me a little more about this," Granddad said. "I'd like to know what-all we got ahead of us."

Mr. Burris seemed a little nervous. "That's hard to say," he said. "The first thing, you've got to send somebody out here with a can of kerosene to burn this carcass. I'd like to kick Mr. Garrett's butt for cutting that animal open. It was the very one thing he ought not to have done. Then you-all better get your cattle together. If you could get them all where we can see them in the morning, it sure would help. We've got to take a lot of samples."

"What kind of samples?" Granddad said. He was watching the vet awful close.

"Samples of this germ," Mr. Burris said. "You see, there's three kinds of this hoof-and-mouth, or anyway, three diseases that look an awful lot alike. One kind just works on cattle, and that's what we hope you haven't got. Another kind works on horses and cattle, and another kind on swine and a few other animals. All of them are bad enough, but of course the cattle and sheep variety is the one where there's the most danger of an epidemic. What we'll have to do is bring a few sheep and a horse or two and some swine and try to give them what this heifer had. We may have to infect a few of

59

your cattle artificially; then we just have to wait and see what happens."

"Well, Mister Burris," Granddad said. "Supposing it turns out to be this epidemic kind, then what? What do you do for it?"

Mr. Burris licked his lips. "I was hoping you knew that," he said, "so I wouldn't have to tell you. I was thinking you'd probably read about some of the other epidemics they've had."

"Oh, I guess I have," Granddad said slowly, his eyes on the stick he was whittling. "But it's been several years ago. I ain't tried to keep up. You mean they still kill cattle for things like that?"

"If it's hoof-and-mouth they do," the vet said. "They don't have any choice. Oh, in European countries they try to stop it with a quarantine, but over here we don't dare do that. In the last bad epidemic in the United States, if I remember correctly, the government had to kill about 77,000 cattle, plus almost that many sheep and goats, and even something like 20,000 deer. It's a terrible thing."

"You mean there ain't no vaccine?" Granddad said. "Ain't you college fellers figured out no better method than killing, in all this time?" He sat with his knife still in his hand, waiting.

"Mr. Bannon, we don't make miracles at college," the vet said. "We don't even know for sure what causes this disease, and you nearly have to know the cause before you can find the cure."

"Then tell me this," Granddad said. "How long will it take to find out just which one of these diseases killed this heifer?"

"If we get to work tomorrow, it shouldn't take longer than a week for the symptoms to begin to show up in the animals we infect. If they don't show up in the horses or the swine in that length of time, then we'll know."

"I see," Granddad said. "Now suppose it is this worst kind, but suppose just a few of my cattle have got it. What then?"

"I'm sorry," the vet said. "One or all, it would still require the same treatment. And incidentally, while we're making the experiment diagnosis, we'll have to insist on a very strict quarantine. No animals of any kind ought to leave this ranch, and no new animals will be allowed to come on it. This disease spreads like a grass fire. So far as we know, we may have it on our clothes right now, or the wind may have blown some of it fifty miles away since Garrett cut that heifer open. Actually, one animal can infect a whole area. And the sad thing is, the disease itself will hardly ever kill an animal—I guess that heifer was one exception— but just let there be a hint of it and you have to kill every head of cattle that's had any contact with it."

"And you're convinced, are you?" Granddad said. "You think that's what killed her?"

"Yes, sir, I do," the vet said.

Granddad stood up and slowly knocked the dust and the mesquite shavings off his pants legs. "Well, sir," he said, "I'll tell you something right now. I'll have my cattle together by tomorrow, as many of them as I can get. I'll help you examine 'em, I'll quarantine 'em, I'll work with you ever way I can. But I won't let you kill this herd, disease or no disease. I'll fence up tight and hold the quarantine as long as you want me to, but I won't let you drive these cattle into pits and shoot 'em, like they do in Mexico. I know, I've heard about it, and what's more I've seen it done. And I don't doubt an epidemic is a terrible thing. But the cattle I saw killed were sick, an' my cattle ain't. Oh, a few of 'em may be, but not many, and it'll take more than a telegram from Austin to convince me they are. I don't doubt I'm contrary and old-fashioned, and wrong about a lot of things, but I don't intend to have my cattle shot out from under me on account of no schoolbook disease. I don't believe in shootin' healthy animals. There's few enough as it is."

The man Thompson laughed when Granddad said that. He seemed to think it was pretty funny. Granddad turned to him, his old neck set.

"What kind of a smart aleck are you, mister?" he said. Thompson's laugh died off, and we all stood there uneasily. Finally Mr. Burris stood up and lifted his bag.

"Well, I don't think we need to talk any more about it today, one way or the other," he said. "I hope it turns out to be one of the minor varieties myself, so we won't ever have to talk about it any more." But it was easy to see he didn't think it would. Going back, Jesse rode with me and Thompson, and he got out to help me shut the hard gate.

2.

When we got back to the barn, Granddad went up to put in a telephone call to the hospital, to see how Grandma was getting along. He sent Jesse and me over to Hank Hutch's place, to see if Hank could help us round the cattle. If we were going to have all the stock in the horse pasture by night, we would need a lot of help, and a fair amount of luck to boot.

I drove, and Jesse slumped over against the door, fiddling with a package of cigarettes. He hadn't shaved that morning, and sweat was shining under the scraggly stubble on his thin cheeks. We were halfway to Hank's before he said a word.

"Looks like I landed in the goddamn wrong place agin," he said sadly. "Trouble's my middle name."

"I don't think it'll turn out so bad," I said. I didn't. Granddad wouldn't let people do anything on his ranch that he wasn't willing to allow.

Jesse sighed. "You got more cherry in your cheeks than I have," he said. "Shit, I can see it building. I oughta stayed on that truck and let it haul me clear to Wyoming."

I turned the pickup off the highway, across the shaky wooden cattle guard, and drove up to Hank's front door. There wasn't a fence, and there wasn't any yard. We saw Hank around to the side of the house, tinkering with an old tractor he'd swapped for somewhere. He waved at us, and came over. He was a tall, red-headed man, built heavy. The paint had worn off the old farmhouse where he and his family were living, and the whole place looked like it was held together with baling wire. There was a broken tricycle standing in the bare flower beds. One of its pedals lay on the porch, with a couple of cracked sawdust dolls.

"I tell you," Hank said, when Jesse had told him what was coming off. "I got one little piece of fixin' to do on a well. It won't take me fifteen minutes. You-all go on and leave me a horse in the lot. I'll catch up with you. I'm ready to start right now." When he wasn't in a hurry, Hank was a lot of fun to fool around with. He turned to the house. "Mama," he said loudly. His wife came then and stood in the door, a thin blond-headed woman with a feed-sack dishcloth in her hands. Hank's three barefoot kids, all of them little girls, hung back behind her, too timid to show themselves while we were in the yard. "I'll be seeing you tonight," Hank said. "Homer's got some work to do, so I guess I'll eat over at the big house." Mrs. Hutch looked like she was worn nearly out; besides the kids she had her mother to take care of. The little girls were as quick to hide as lizards.

"You-all come in an' have some ice tea before you go off in the hot," she said.

"Naw, we can't, Mama," Hank said. "Homer's got about three day's work to get done by sundown." He started for his pickup. "I'll go in mine," he said. "See you fellers in the pasture."

As I started back up the road I could see the three little blond-headed girls standing on Hank's front porch, watching us drive off.

"Ain't that a hell of a way to live?" Jesse said. "I pity that pore woman."

I couldn't understand why Jesse was so depressed. It seemed like he always felt sorrier for people than they felt for themselves. I guess he was probably feeling the sorriest for himself, all the time. Hank and Janine had a pretty hard time of it, all right, but they always seemed fairly cheerful, and acted like they got along pretty good. Hank was as jolly as the next man, poor or not. But Jesse sat in his corner, silent and sulking about it, while I drove home. I turned on the radio a minute and heard "Driftwood on the River" before we came to the ranch. When we drove through the cattle guard we saw Granddad and Lonzo standing down at the lots. They had their chaps on and their horses saddled, ready to go. Jesse came out of it a little.

"That sure is a nice pony your Granddad rides,"

he said. He meant Stranger, Granddad's pride and
joy. Halmea was out in the back yard hanging out a
washing—when I honked at her she dropped a
couple of clothespins. I parked the pickup in the
shady hallway of the barn, and we walked out into
the hot dusty sunlight, to catch our horses and
begin the round.

CHAPTER

4

We spent the rest of that morning riding through the hot, weedy pastures, pushing the cows and calves out of the shady places where they were resting. It was after eight o'clock when we started—a bad time of day to be working cattle, hot as it was—but we took it as easy as we could. Granddad had four little pastures, and one big one. His old cows had been fed all winter and were gentle as they could be; it was just a matter of finding them in the brush and throwing them together. Once we got them in bunches they were easy enough to handle. Hank Hutch caught up with us before we had the first pasture rounded, and with him helping we got along a lot faster. As we loped through the high weeds in the valley pastures the weed pollen swirled up around us and started us sneezing.

By dinnertime we were driving the cows from the third little pasture up the hill toward the house. Our horses were lathered from the morning's ride, and all the cattle were too hot. The little calves had their tongues out, dripping long white strings of slobber into the dust. Every minute or two the old cows would try to stop and graze. We were about as hot and droopy as the cattle, our Levis sweated through, and our khaki shirts looking like they'd come through a washing machine without being wrung out dry. The cattle drifted into the big horse-pasture tank, and we rode to the barn. "Let's turn these ponies loose," Granddad said. "We'll start fresh this afternoon." We pitched our saddles in the shade and watched the horses roll around, scratching their sweaty withers in the dirt.

When we got to the house, a washpan full of cool water was sitting on the porch table, with a cake of lye soap beside it, and a handy towel. Lonzo washed up first and sat down on the concrete steps to clean his fingernails. In a minute Halmea called us in to eat.

Granddad was slow coming up from the barn. He came in after the rest of us had already sat down at the table. "Take your time an' eat," he said. "You may not get another chance to rest till after dark." He looked shaggy and solemn, and pretty tired.

So we ate. Halmea had earned her money that morning, if she never did again. She had beans and steak and flour gravy, tomatoes and onions and lettuce and radishes from the garden, some fried okra, some hominy, hot rolls and butter, and cherry cobbler for dessert. It looked like an awful lot of food when we set down to it, but with Lonzo and Hank sitting across the table from one another it sure melted away. The rest of us ate our share, but we were just amateurs compared to them. When we were done all the bowls were empty, and the cherry cobbler was just a red stain in the bottom of a piepan. Halmea poured another round of ice tea, and we loosened our belts. Granddad got up the minute he was finished and carried his plate to the kitchen.

"You-all drink your tea and rest a minute," he said. "I got to make a phone call."

"He shore looks down in the mouth," Hank said, when Granddad had gone on out of hearing. "You don't reckon they'll really come in here with the guns, do you?" He looked at Jesse.

Jesse let a thin cloud of smoke case out of his nose before he answered. "I've heard of it happenin'," he said.

"If a man come on my land and told me something like what that vet told Mister Homer, there'd be a quick war," Lonzo said. "I remember when they first started this cotton measurin' business. Some old boy come out an' told Pa he couldn't plant but so much cotton. Pa said he'd plant what he pleased, and the feller kept on him till he finally went and got the shotgun. The old boy left, but it didn't do Pa no good. He ended up just plantin' so much cotton anyway, and the fuckin' grasshoppers ate two thirds of that."

Granddad called for us to come on, and we all got up. I was just a tiny bit stiff from the morning's ride. We picked up our straw hats and stepped out into the yard, where the sky was white with sun and heat. I stepped under the sycamore tree a minute, to adjust my eyes.

"This evenin's gonna be a regular bitch," Jesse said, pulling the brim of his hat down a little farther. He had got in the habit of dreading things. We left the cool sycamore shade and went down to the lots to catch our horses. I led mine to the big water trough and let him drink his fill. He was a worthless, long-legged bay horse that I didn't much like. The water in the trough was deep and black near the bottom, with little green patches of mossy scum floating on the surface. When we mounted, the sky was high and white, with just a few thin milkweed clouds scattered near the horizons. The horses were sweating before we had gone a mile.

But the rounding that afternoon went better than any of us had expected it to. We were lucky in the big pasture, and found most of the cows in one place, so we didn't have to waste so much time prowling in the heavy mesquite thickets. They were standing around in the shade, but we stirred them up and pushed them down the brown sandy trails to a tank. The old cows waded in up to their bellies, while the big half-yearling calves farted around on the banks. When we got them all started toward the house Granddad sent Hank and me off to look for those that were missing. I rode my bay hard for a couple of hours, trotting along the brown shelving ridges and shoving through the thick weeds and the blooming green mesquites in the flats. I found two little bunches of cattle and managed to get them to the main herd before it left the pasture, so I felt fairly proud of myself. By five o'clock we had them trailing into the horse-pasture tank. Granddad sent Hank and Lonzo to get a pickup load of hay, to scatter for the cattle, and he and Jesse and I got fresh horses and loped down the road a couple of miles to the little Idiot Ridge pasture, the last one we had to round.

The pasture was open, not many trees on it, and compared to some of the others it was easy gathered. It was our bad luck that all the cattle were on the far side, standing around the windmill, so we had a long drive to make by dark. It was beginning to cool off a little, but Granddad kept his oldest cows in the Idiot Ridge country, and with them we couldn't make much time. Right at sundown we were driving them along the high ridge toward headquarters, with another mile and a half to go. In front of us the red sun was dropping cleanly down the last few feet of sky, falling into the gold thicket of mesquite on the far hill. There was not a cloud near it, nothing to break the clear spread of light.

The pasture lay under the quietest, stillest light of day; it looked as perfect as some ranch picture on a serum calendar. The old cows walked slowly, their red coats gray to the flank with dust, their heads low. Now and then they stopped so a calf could suck a swallow or two of milk before we prodded them on. Some of them still carried their calves. Their sides bulged like barrels, and streams of yellow piss trickled down their hindquarters into the grass and dirt. The little calves waddled along stiff-legged, bawling for their mothers to stop. The old Hereford bull and the two longhorn steers, the cattle that Granddad kept for old time's sake, were in the herd. The two rangy, brindle steers walked in the front, following the trail down the long slope to the lots. The old bull slouched along behind, twitching the black buzz flies off his back. We all fell back to the rear and let the cattle follow the steers—they knew where they were going as well as we did. The evening air was cool, but heavy with the smells of dust and cattle piss and prairie weed. The grass was already browning under the long days of sun. Before us the trail ran downward like a slack lariat rope, ending at the big water trough.

Granddad was tired; he sat loose in his saddle. "I swear," he said. "I wonder if the government's gonna inspect them two longhorns of mine. They're gonna have a time adoin' it. Them big horns'll never go through a chute."

"Where'd you get them two?" Jesse asked.

"Raised 'em," Granddad said. "I been keeping 'em to remind me how times was. Cattle like them make me feel like I'm in the cattle business."

"Hell, I'd let 'em go back in the brush," Jesse said. "Then if the government wants 'em, let the government go find 'em."

"Well, I don't know what to think yet," Granddad said. "I ain't gonna try to decide till I find out for sure what's wrong with my cattle." He spit tobacco juice into the grass. "Don't do no good to worry ahead," he said. "Anyway, I guess I know now what's the matter with that case of sore-foot we got up in the hospital trap. I didn't think that looked much like the foul-foot."

Then we drove the tired cattle through the twilight, and he said no more. We got them to the tank just about the time the new moon lifted its rim above the highway to the east, a big swollen grapefruit of a moon. The cows walked out into the water, but the two big steers stopped and began to tear and shake the blocks of hay that Lonzo and Hank had scattered. We left them there, drinking and eating, pushing in with cattle from the other pastures, and I thought of how much work it would take to get them all separated again. That was enough to put me down on the government myself. After I unsaddled I left Granddad and the men to make plans for the morning, and went on to the house. I wanted to clean up as quick as I could, and get into Thalia for a little while, to shoot some pool.

I thought maybe if I got to Halmea when nobody was around, she could help me come up with an excuse.

Halmea turned out to be a help, all right. She figured up what groceries we needed, and it didn't take much to persuade Granddad to let me go in after them. I bathed and put on some clean Levis and a T-shirt before I ate; then as soon as I was through eating I got in the pickup and drove away from the ranch, through the cool night. As I left I saw Jesse and Lonzo sitting on the steps of the bunkhouse; I didn't much want them to go, and I didn't figure they much wanted to, so I didn't ask them. I drove slow till I got out of the horse pasture, so as not to bump the old cows that stood in the road.

When I got to the highway I turned my little window in and let the cool air swoosh on me as I gunned the old pickup toward Thalia. Just inside the city limits I braked and swung off the pavement onto the crunching gravel driveway of the highway grocery store. I thought I had better get the groceries first, before the old people who ran the store went to bed. A couple of old women were rocking on the porch, in front of the R. C. Cola thermometers and the Garrett snuff signs. I bought some bread and sugar, picked myself up a new pair of work gloves, twirled the paperback rack a time or two, and went out. I had the night to play around with, what there was of it between then and getting-up time.

Thalia was a still, quiet place at night. I drove slowly through the one long main street, now and then hearing a snatch of fiddle music out some open window. Some of the folks were out watering their lawns or visiting with the neighbors. In the summertime, in that country, evening is the peaceful time of day.

I parked on the square and got out. In front of me, under the big courthouse mulberry trees, a few old men were sitting on the wooden benches, talking and whittling and spitting as the night came down. Those old men were always there. On Saturday afternoons when I was younger I used to dirty up my clean weekend Levis, sitting on the ground in the mashed mulberries, listening to the old men swap stories and yarns. But after a while their talk got old. All they knew were stories about old times, and I could hear better ones than they could tell from Granddad. They sat there then, they sit there now, I guess, whittling, spitting, nothing for them but the benches and the mulberry mush, the whittle sticks and the Brown Mule. But it was getting later, and I knew that pretty soon they would wobble home to their daughters' back rooms and leave the square to we boys.

There were a lot of kids in the pool hall, standing around the eight-ball tables at the back, Cokes and cues in their hands. My buddy Hermy Neal was at one table, shooting eight-ball with a cousin who was visiting him from Oklahoma City. I skirted around the money tables, where the reckless-ass oil drillers were shooting nine-ball at a dollar a throw. They were studs, those drillers: all they cared about was their cars and their work, and now and then their gambling. Dumb Billy, the stupid orphan kid who made what living he had shoveling shit at the local stock pens, was standing by a snooker table. He liked to watch the balls roll across the smooth green felt. Lem the Lion, the old nigger who ran the pool hall, was slipping around with his rack waiting for the games to be over so he could take in money.

"Hey, man," Hermy said. "You got your pickup?"

"It's on the square," I said. "Who's takin' the winner?"

"Winner's ass," he said. "Let's go get some beer while we got transportation." He was a tall blackheaded kid, fairly devil-may-care. He was a pretty good athlete when he wanted to be.

I hadn't meant to go out of town that night, but the more I thought about it the better idea it seemed. And I didn't really ponder it long. Granddad would be too sound asleep to know when I came in. He hardly ever knew anyway.

"I'm game," I said, watching Hermy's four-eyed cousin draw a bead on the four-ball. He hit it head on and missed the pocket about a foot and a half.

"Table's off level," he said. "Look at it wobble."

"You fucked up," Hermy said. He grinned and bradded in the eight-ball. His cousin drug a dime out of his pocket and pitched it on the table for

Lem the Lion. Then he and I and Hermy and a couple more boys cut out and piled in the pickup.

"Make the square a time or two," Hermy said. "We might scare up some pussy."

"You're dreamin', man," his cousin said. His cousin thought Thalia was a shitheap of a town, and he was always putting up Oklahoma City. "You could circle this goddamn square a thousand times and not see a good-lookin' girl," he said.

"Who said good-lookin'?" Hermy said. "I wouldn't back away from a gentle heifer, not tonight." He wouldn't, either. It hadn't been long since half the boys in the town had had a wild soiree with a blind heifer, out on a creek one cold night.

But it turned out the cousin was right. I blew out of town and we flew down the road toward the county line, laughing and fighting in the cab, weaving all over the road sometimes. We were all too young to buy beer, but that didn't matter. If no cops were around the clerk would sell to a six-year-old, and if some were close by you had to look like Granddad even to get inside the store. Hermy's cousin was the littlest fart in the pickup, but we made him go in. He had to prove he wasn't completely worthless. Actually, the man would have sold him the store if he'd had any money.

On the way back to Thalia we tore into the six-packs. Hermy was an expert at opening the cans so they'd spew right in somebody's face, and he gave his cousin a regular beer bath. His cousin was so excited he didn't mind. We were living it up for once, talking about where we might find some girls when we got back.

But when we got there the drive-ins were closed, and the only person awake in the whole town, it looked like, was old Buttermilk, the night watchman. He was sitting on the curb in front of the grocery store, talking to his scroungy brown dog. There was nothing to do but make the lover's lanes, and then drive around the square and the two business blocks while we finished the beer.

"Shit, let's get out, man," the cousin said. We were all tired of riding, so we took the rest of our beer and went over to the courthouse benches to drink it. In a few minutes Buttermilk shambled over, beginning his rounds. "You boys ain't jackin' off, are you?" he asked. That was his favorite question. We hurrahed him a little and he went on. The moon was high and the courthouse lawn was white with light. We watched the one stoplight turn from red to green, from green to red, from red to green, and on and on.

"I'm horny," Hermy said. He was sitting in the grass fiddling with an empty beer can.

"I wish we could go someplace," I said. "I'd like to go to Fort Worth or someplace like that."

"I don't want no Fort Worth," Hermy said. He was trying to bend the can between his hands. "I just want some pussy in the next half hour or so."

His cousin snorted. He was getting pretty drunk,

and his glasses had slipped way down on his nose. He looked like he was going to get sick on the beer.

"You boys don't know what it is," he said. "You oughta live in Oklahoma City. Man, up there you have to fight to keep your pants on." He thought he was pretty much of a cocksman.

"Is that how you got so rough?" Buddy said. Buddy was a little guy, but he always acted mean and hustly. If he got his bluff in on somebody he'd run them ragged.

"That's how," the cousin said. "How you been making out with the milk cows?" He was a little drunk and a good deal excited. "Man, this town is nowhere," he said. "Nowhere, U.S.A. Deadass County, Texas." Everybody had been pestering him for days, and he was getting back.

"By god, I wondered how you got so tough," Buddy said.

"I'm not the roughest," the cousin said, pushing his glasses back up in place. "But I know damn well I can whip your ass," he said, taking his glasses off.

We all perked up a little. It wouldn't be much fight, but at least something would be happening.

"You got it to whip," Buddy said.

Both of them were too full of beer to have good sense, and too far gone to back down. They went out in the moonlight to fight, being careful to pick a spot of lawn where there weren't any water faucets to trip over. When they found one they began to stand and look at one another, with their fists doubled up.

"Start it, you chickenshit," Buddy said. He was in his Golden Gloves crouch, but he didn't move toward the cousin.

"You start it," the cousin said. "I'll end it."

Hermy was so disgusted with the whole thing he didn't even get up off the grass. I felt kinda sorry for the two, actually—it was half funny and half sad, the way they kept walking around and around one another in the moonlight. Neither one was mad at the other, really, and they must have both been wondering how they ended up in such a fix. Finally Buddy got his nerve up enough to run in and hit at the cousin, and they had a little shove fight that lasted about ten shoves. Then they separated and stood there, trying to get chummy so they wouldn't have to fight any more.

Hermy got up off the ground and knocked the dirt off his ass. "I'm going home before I get killed," he said. I took him and the cousin home and left Buddy and the others on the square, to talk over the fight. As I drove out of town I noticed the rodeo flags waving in the breeze: the Thalia rodeo was less than a week away. I felt blue as I drove out the empty highway. The silly fight had put me in a lonesome mood, and I couldn't get the funny, beery feeling out of my stomach. I turned on the radio and got some hillybilly music, but it didn't cheer me up. I wouldn't have minded going with Hermy's cousin to see what it was like in Oklahoma City, at least it would be a change. Thalia was okay, I really liked it, but I just didn't want it for all the time. The old cows bawling in the horse pasture kept me awake till nearly morning, and I lay in bed with my eyes open, thinking about all the girls I knew in Thalia, and those in Oklahoma City I didn't know, all of them with nightgowns on, asleep somewhere and breathing in the night.

CHAPTER
_____ 5 _____

1.

The early sun shone on Stranger's sorrel coat, and when he moved his head to look at Mr. Burris, the curb chain on the bridle jingled a little. Granddad had gotten off, to talk, but the rest of us were still on horseback, waiting for orders. The sun was less than half an hour high, but we had already made a circle of the horse pasture, and all the cattle were milling and stirring up dust in the big pen. Mr. Burris stood in front of us, slapping his gloves against his leg. He had shown up that morning in a station wagon, with four men besides Thompson, and a lot of veterinary equipment.

"I think while you've got 'em all penned I'll just have you run 'em all through the chute," he said to Granddad. "If it won't be too much trouble. That way we can kinda get an idea of how many's infected, and how far along they are. Then we can get what specimens we need without any trouble."

"I see," Granddad said. He had shaved that morning, and had on a clean shirt and a fresh blue pair of Levis. "That'll be fine with us. When you-all get done with 'em we may work a few of these calves, if that ain't against the law."

"No, sir," Mr. Burris said. "You do what you want to with 'em. We're ready to get to work if you are."

We all turned our horses and rode into the dusty lots. First we separated into two lines of horsemen and let the cattle trickle between us, so we could count them. Then we cut them up into groups, the cows that had calves in one place, the drys in another, the yearlings someplace else. Hank and Jesse and one or two of the neighbors went on with the separating, while Lonzo and I tied our horses and began to run the oldest cows through the squeeze chute so the vets could work on them. Cecil Goad, one of our neighbors, would run a few cows into a little crowding pen, and then it was up to me and Lonzo to put them on in the chute. The vets were waiting. They were all dressed in gray coats, and had a whole conglomeration of bottles and jars set out beside the chute. They turned out to be a quiet, hard-working bunch; they handled their end of it a lot quicker and smoother than Lonzo and I handled ours. It was a mean, tiresome job, any way you went at it. The chute was plenty big enough for calves, but it was a pretty tight squeeze for some of the old cows, and we had the devil of a time getting them to take it. We couldn't get but ten or twelve in the pen at one bunch, and then they spun and kicked and bellered, started in the chute and backed out, stuck their heads in the corners and wouldn't move, turned and snorted, did ever aggravating thing they could think of to do. In a few minutes Lonzo and I were covered with dust, and hoarse from yelling at the old cows. The sun got high and the dust rose in a cloud from the sandy pens as the cattle milled and bawled. Granddad was working at the head of the chute, letting the cattle out when the vets were done.

It was past the middle of the morning before we had a real breakdown, but when it came it was a good one. Three cows got to crawling on top of one another in the chute and busted one fence to smithereens. Once it was busted there wasn't anything we could do but stop and fix it, and that took till nearly dinnertime. So when we went up to eat we hadn't even finished with the cows, and had all the calves and yearlings to work that afternoon. We ate quick and started in again, in the white heat of twelve-thirty. I was loggy, too full of ice tea and pie, and it got me into trouble. We had the crowding pen almost empty, just one old cow left in it. She was a thin line-backed hussy, with one horn broken off and a long string of foamy slobber hanging from her chin; nothing we could do would make her take the chute. We surrounded her and finally she stuck her head in like she meant to go. When she did I run up behind her to shut the gate. Then she turned back through herself like a bobcat and went charging down the west wall of the pen. As she went by me she threw out a big cracked hoof, and I spun away from it like I had from a thousand others. Only I spun a fraction too slow, and it caught me on the hip. All I felt was a shove, and a splat on my chaps. When I tuned in on things again I was outside the pen, sitting with my back against the red plank railing of the scales, and Granddad was wiping my forehead with a piece of wet cotton he had got from one of the vets. Inside the pens the dust was still swirling.

"You all right, son?" Granddad asked me. He poured some cold water over the cotton and rubbed my head. "She kicked you into the fence," he said. "You skint your head a little on the pipe."

He seemed to think I would survive, because he handed me the cotton and went back to the head of the chute. My head was throbbing a little, but my hip wasn't sore. While I was trying to make up my mind to get up, Mr. Burris came and knelt down by the water can to pour himself a drink.

"Boy, you caught a lick," he said, smiling at me. "That woulda killed an old man like me."

I didn't feel very talkative, so I just nodded and gave a kind of sickly grin. He sat there a minute, trying to be friendly, but neither of us could think of anything to say. Finally he put the lid back on the water can and left, and I got up and went back to the crowding pen. I knew the cowboys would be on me for a week if I quit work because of a little skint head.

And I could have worked anywhere but in that crowding pen, heat or skint head or not. It was about two o'clock in the afternoon, hellish hot weather, and all of us were sweat and dust over sweat, and more sweat trickling through the fresh coat of dust. Little branches and creeks and streams of sweat ran out from under our shirtsleeves and hatbands, and there were dark muddy brown spots in the circles of dirt under our eyes. The pen was like a sand pile with a monstrous fan in the bottom, blowing the sand up into our faces; then when it got so high the hot south wind blew it back down our necks. We were working the heifers by then, all of them scary as antelope and about as wild. Lonzo had got his hands on an electric hotshot, and the way he was jobbing the heifers could have got us all killed; it just made the cattle spin and kick that much worse. After about an hour of sucking in dirt and spitting mud I got sick to my stomach, and while we were bringing in a new penful of calves my dinner came up in a burning gush, most of it through my nose. I gagged and gagged, and my head kept throbbing, the sweat that stung the raw place just making it worse. I started to go back in the pen, and then I thought fuck it and went to the house, the weak trembles so bad in my legs I was afraid I was going to flop in the path, right there in the red ants and chickenshit.

When I hobbled in the back door, Halmea was in the kitchen rolling out a piecrust. She took one look at me and came over and grabbed my arm.

"Honey, you's white as a sheet," she said. "Sit down heah."

"Leave me alone," I said. "No wonder I'm white, you got flour all over me."

"Okay," she said, turning me loose. "Go splat on de flooah, see who picks you up." I saw her brush her hair back with one hand, leaving a white streak of flour across her forehead. I went on up the stairs and flopped on my counterpane, feeling sick and sleepy. My room was hot as a cookstove, and in a little while I came out of a doze, lathering in a pool of my own sweat, my head about to crack open. In the white, still heat I could hear the cattle bawling from the lots. I thought how much better it would have been if we'd ridden that day—at least, riding, there were breezes along the ridgetops, and the sweat cooled as it trickled down your ribs. In the bed it was close and sticky. I dozed again, still conscious of the oven of heat, and the constant pulsing in my temples. Then I looked up and Halmea was in the room; she was setting something on my little bedside table. I saw her through a dozy haze, standing over me, the white band of flour on her forehead moistened with sweat and running a little. She said something that I didn't understand, and stopped to feel my forehead with her cool hand. When she stooped I saw part of her breasts. I didn't say anything, and in a minute she left the room. I raised up and found a big glass of sweetened lemonade on my table, the sugar just settling to the bottom. The cold glass was sweating, and the lemonade was pale, full of thin chips of ice. I sat up and drank it slowly, sipping the sweetened juice and spitting the white seeds across the room in the direction of the wastebasket. Then I fished out the thin, melting slivers of ice and sucked them one at a time, to make them last. I thought how much nicer it was to be drinking Halmea's lemonade than to be chowsing cattle in the dusty pens. Halmea was good about some things; she was good, period. If she was in the mood she would take care of you whether you wanted her to or not. Right then I liked her as well or better than almost anyone I knew. As I sucked the ice, I thought of her in my room, remembering the white on her forehead and the dark slope of her breasts against her seersucker dress. When I had finished the ice I let the sugared water in the bottom of the glass slide over my tongue, and then I sat the glass on the table and slept again, a longer, cooler sleep.

2.

Granddad's hand on my shoulder woke me. The yard was shadowy with twilight, and at first I thought I had slept on through the night. "Don't you want some supper, son?" he asked. He was sitting on the thrown-back quilt that lay across the foot of my bed. From the mask of muddy dust on his face I knew he had just come from the lots. "Get up an' wash an' eat a bite," he said. "You'll feel better." His voice was tired and slow, but powerful with feeling, and he lifted one of his stubby hands from the quilt and ran it through his stiff dusty hair. I looked out the window, into the evening. Three scissortails were chasing a raggedy-winged old crow across the sky. The horizon to the west was still rosy, but the sun was long gone for that day. Granddad stood up, and I saw that the sweat of the long day had soaked through his Levis and darkened the leather of his wide, hand-made belt. "Pretty evenin', but it was a shitter of a day," he said. "Hud and his momma ought to be in before too long." He left, and I sat up in bed, tired from sleeping too long.

By the time I got downstairs, full dark had come to the plains. I stood on the back porch a minute, smelling the grassy evening smells of the country. Jesse and Lonzo were eating when I went in. They were too worked down to do much more than nod. Halmea came in with a stewer full of cold apricot preserves. "You alive, or is you a ghost?" she said.

"I bet his appetite'd be the last thing to die," Granddad said. I was pretty hungry, but I didn't feel like talking. Lonzo was so tired he kept dozing off with his coffee cup halfway to his mouth, and sloshing coffee on his wrists. He stumbled off to the bunkhouse right after supper, but me and Jesse went out and set on the cellar while Jesse smoked.

"You pretty tired?" I said.

"You better believe it," he said. "I can't take work like I used to. Rodeoin' so long got me outa shape for anything else. I'm too tired even to sleep.

Maybe if I sit here a minute I can get up the energy to go to bed."

"How is it rodeoin'?" I said. "Isn't it pretty excitin'?"

He lit another cigarette and shook out the match. "For a while it's excitin'," he said. "Then it just gets to be work. It ain't like workin' out here, plain cowboyin', but it's still work."

I was hoping he'd go on and tell me about some of his high times, but he didn't seem like he wanted to talk. Jesse was that way. Whenever I was just aching for him to talk, he wouldn't say two words. It was when I'd just as soon be quiet and think that he thought of so many things to tell. I guess we coulda been wonderful friends if we coulda got together at the right times a little more often.

We sat on the sloping stone roof of the cellar and were quiet. The moon was above us to the southwest, like a round white slice of pear. I could hear rock 'n' roll music from the kitchen radio, just loud enough that I could enjoy it without especially listening. In a few minutes the light clicked out in the kitchen and I heard the slap of Halmea's loose sandals on the concrete of the back porch. She stopped in the yard and stood in front of us, still tapping one foot to the turned-off music.

"You-all come play me some checkahs," she said. "Some marble checkahs. Come on, Lonnie, you fresh outa anything to do."

"Okay," I said, standing up. "Sure, I'll come

clean your plow." She asked Jesse to come too, but he stomped out his cigarette and shook his head.

"I couldn't even see the marble holes, I'm so tired," he said. The three of us walked out of the yard, down the trail toward the bunkhouse. The trail was a pale rope of light between the dark patches of weeds. The old cows had been driven back to the pastures, and there was no bawling that night, just the singing crickets.

"Last time I played checkers was before my Grandpa died," Jesse said.

"I enjoy playin' dis Chinese," Halmea said. She was afraid of snakes, walking so close to me that she stepped on my heels about every yard or so. "I gets tiredsome workin' all de time."

We weren't even to Halmea's cabin when I heard the roar of a car on the dirt road. "Whoa," I said. "Guess who's comin' now?" I could almost see Hud gunning the Lincoln over the graded road. Granny would be sitting up straight as a poker in the seat, waiting to tear into us.

"I might know," Halmea said. "Be no checkah playin' tonight. I bettah least get de coffeepot on." She turned and started quickly back toward the house.

"Maybe the operation will slow the old lady down a little," Jesse said. "Make her ease up."

Up the trail, Halmea heard what he said, and her quick deep laugh came back to us through the darkness. "She didn't have any operation," I said.

"It was all just in her mind to begin with. She complained so much Granddad decided to send her down for a put-up treatment. All they did was put her to sleep and take a few fake stitches. She's no worse off than she's ever been."

"Well, I've heard 'em all, now," Jesse said. "I sure nough better get some sleep."

I stood in the dark, listening to the sound of the car. I heard the pipes on the cattle guard rattle; Hud must have hit it doing about sixty-five. The car lights lashed against the trees in the back yard, and he hit the brakes and burned gravel right up to the gate. By the time I got to the car Hud had Grandma out and was carrying her through the back yard, her fussing ever step of the way. I loaded myself with boxes and kicked the car door shut; the radio was still on, but I would have had to set my load down to turn it off. Hud met me at the back door, his old self. He was chewing a toothpick to splinters, and his tangled black hair looked like it hadn't been combed since he left.

"Time you got here," he said. "Ma wants a nightgown outa one a them boxes; you better take it to her. She thinks she's done a hard day's work, sittin' on her butt talkin' a blue streak for three hundred miles."

I stumbled on into the kitchen with my load, but I almost dropped it when I saw Halmea. She was bent over the kitchen table, crying, the tears running down her wrists and dripping onto the white oilcloth. I was so surprised I didn't stop, I went on to Grandma's room, wondering what in the world had happened to spoil Halmea's good mood. Granny was sitting on the edge of her bed, fanning and talking out loud to herself.

"Sit them luggages down," she said. "Get me my blue sleepers outa that yeller box. I got to get still befo' this heat an' all gives me a relapse." She was tickled to death to have me to talk at. "Never in my life was I in anything like that hospital," she said. "Them places is just one sin right after another. A person'd be better off just to stay home an' trust in the Lord." I wasn't finding any blue sleepers, and I was wanting to go see what had happened to Halmea. Granny never let up. "One a them nurses, tryin' to undress me bare as a baby with menfolks in the room, I told that hussy. Shame an' disgrace." I finally found a gray nightgown in another box, and I pitched it to her.

"Where I told you to look in the first place," she said.

Halmea was still sitting at the table, wiping her eyes with a soggy paper napkin. She was holding her breast with one hand. When she saw me come in she dropped her hand and looked down. Every second or two her chest would jerk, like she had the hiccups. There was beans and meat on the table for Hud, but he wasn't there.

"What's the matter, Halmea?" I said. "You want me to go get you anything?"

She shook her head, her eyes filling up and her mouth quivering. "If dey was, it'd be a gun," she said, her voice shaky. She wouldn't say another word. I saw she just wanted me to get out, so I left.

There was a light flashing in the front yard and I went around to see about it. It was Hud, poking around under the hood of his convertible with the big flashlight. He was whistling "The Wabash Cannonball," and fiddling with his fan belt.

"Here," he said. "Hold this light a minute. I want to check them batteries."

"Did you see what was the matter with Halmea?" I said. "She wasn't crying when you-all came in, was she?"

"Let me have the light," he said. When I handed it to him he suddenly shined it right in my eyes, so I had to turn my head. Then he slammed the hood with both hands.

"Naw, she wasn't bawlin' when I went in," he said. "I gave her a little tittie squeeze. I guess you're old enough to know how that is, ain't you? A man gets to wantin' a little choclate milk." He got behind the wheel and began to turn the engine over.

I walked around to his window, feeling helpless and mad at the same time. "Goddamn you," I said. "Don't you do that no more."

He snickered. "Fuck off," he said. "You ain't got no private milkin' rights."

He leaned his head out the window and let his motor idle. Neither one of us said anything. "Let me tell you something," he said in a minute. "I heard about this big cattle inspection you-all had today. Me an' that Grandpa a yours is goin' round and round one a these days, and I ain't gonna be the one that get's dizzy." He threw the car in gear suddenly and whipped out onto the road. Before he drove off he laughed and gave me the finger.

I went to the Lincoln and drove it into its shed. Then I got out and set on its back fender awhile, trying to decide what to do about Halmea. I wanted to cheer her up some way, but I probably couldn't manage it if I tried. It wasn't such a dark night, but a lot of small clouds were racing beneath the stars like greyhounds, pushed along by the high south wind. I was half in the mood to go to Thalia, but I didn't.

Finally I walked down to Halmea's shack. It was dark inside, but I didn't figure she was asleep. I stood in front of her door for a few minutes, hoping she would see me through the screen and say something. When I saw she wasn't going to, I walked around to her window. Ever minute or so the moon would come clear between the sliding clouds, and the moonlight shone pale and floury over the shack wall and the whole ranch yard. Her bed was pushed right up against the window screen, and I could make out the whiteness of her cotton nightgown. Ordinarily it would have set me on fire, seeing her on a bed, but then I didn't feel that way. "Halmea," I whispered. I whispered several times, but I had to say it louder before she heard me.

"Who out dere?" she said.

"Me," I said. "I'm sorry I woke you up."

"What you want?" she said. She didn't sound particularly friendly.

"Just to say much obliged for the lemonade," I said. That hadn't occurred to me till that minute, but it sounded good. "That was all."

She didn't say anything for a minute, and then she chuckled and rolled over. "Okay," she said. "Much oblige fo' you goin' on about you rat-killin' and lettin' me sleep."

I did. I went to my room, but it was a long time that night before I went to sleep. I read a little of *From Here to Eternity,* and then lay on my bed wide awake in the darkness, my head full of old sights and half-dreams, some nice and some uneasy. I remembered something Hud had told me once about my daddy: how he had killed my real grandmother. Hud said a snake had crawled up on the cellar, and Daddy shot at it and the bullet ricocheted off and hit Grandmother in the head. Granddad was off in the pasture, and she died under the sycamore tree before he got home. I never had the nerve to ask Granddad about it. But I knew that the ranch wasn't as cheerful as it had been. Hud and Granddad had too many bad arguments, and now there was the cattle disease and all that to worry about. Sometimes reading about Karen Holmes would make me wonder about the army, but I didn't think I would feel like Prew did about it, and I didn't intend to go off the deep end in that direction. Then there was Jesse's gloom and

Halmea's crying and a lot of things that didn't look good.

Sometime late at night Hud came roaring in in his Ford. He stopped it under the shade trees by the back fence. His radio was on good and loud, and from where I lay I could hear Carl Smith singing "The Bonaparte's Retreat." Hud switched the radio off in the middle of a line, and went on singing it himself. He sounded like he had whisky in his voice. I raised on my elbows and watched him stand by the water house cleaning his boots. It was Hud's one good habit, cleaning his boots every time he wore them.

I don't remember seeing him go into the house at all: he may have cleaned them all night. I dozed off about that time, and I dreamed that Granddad and I were out together, riding in the early morning. The sun was just up, and the breeze cool on us as we rode across the high country. We stopped our horses on the edge of a hill, a high, steep hill, maybe it was the cap rock, and rested, our legs across the horses' necks. There below us was Texas, green and brown and graying in the sun, spread wide under the clear spread of sky like the opening scene in a big Western movie. There were rolling hills in the north, and cattle grazing here and there, and strings of horses under the shade trees. Then above us the little gray clouds began to slip away toward the north like coyotes in the pastures. We could see creeks winding across the flats, dark green oak trees growing along their banks. The green waving acres of mesquite spread out and away from us to the south and east. I saw the highways cutting through the bright unshaded towns, and I kept expecting Granddad to say something to me. But he was relaxed, looking across the land. Finally he swung his feet into the stirrups and we rode down together into the valley toward some ranch I couldn't see, the Llano Estacado or the old Matador. . . .

CHAPTER

6

The next morning Granddad woke me up to see if I wanted to go into Wichita with him, to a cattle sale. He had bought some milk cows from a man the week before, and had agreed to get them at the sale. Now that the quarantine was on he couldn't bring them on the ranch, but Hank Hutch had agreed to buy them if Granddad would haul them to his place. I jumped into some clean Levis and got down to breakfast in a hurry, but it was hurry wasted. Hud decided out of contrariness that he wanted to go, and while we were waiting for him to change clothes Grandma got in a preserving mood. The upshot of it was that we all ended up working in the garden till almost ten o'clock, bosses, hired hands, and all. She even had Hud out picking peas in his floosy pants. When we left she and Halmea had a wagonload of produce to put up.

It was past dinnertime, still and hot as could be, when we got to the auction barn. I had planned on stopping off in Wichita and seeing a picture show, but Granddad vetoed that. He said he might not stay long, and he didn't want to have to hunt me up. He was looking tired and depressed, like he wasn't feeling very gay. I figured Hud would give him hell about the cattle and the vets on the way in, but Hud didn't. When we got to the sale Granddad went off to prowl among the pens, looking for the man who had the milk cows, and Hud got with some of his gambling cronies and disappeared into the beer joint next door. I was left by myself to watch the sale, like I knew I'd be.

For a while it was enjoyable. There was a little row of padded seats around the auction ring. They were for the privileged buyers to use, the men who represented big feed lots and packing concerns. They were a mean, crooked lot to my way of thinking, but they were fun to watch. They sat around in gray shirts and $10 straw hats looking proud of themselves. They talked and cussed and guzzled the cold beer the waitresses kept packing in from the stockyards café; but in spite of all the chatter they never missed an animal that came through the ring, and nine times out of ten it was one of them that made the buy. The auctioneer was auction-talking in a steady stream, leaning over the rail with a microphone in his hand, his pearl-buttoned shirt sweated through. Behind the big buyers, wooden grandstands sloped up to the ceiling. The little men sat on them, the small ranchers, talking stock to one another, and the dirt farmers in yellow flat-brimmed hats and blue overalls, come in maybe to sell a milk-pen calf. I saw a big operator walk around the ring, a beer bottle in one hand and a little snap-tail whip in the other. He had on white pigskin gloves, and he stopped all the way around the packer's ring to slap people on the back and interrupt their conversations. The cattle poured through the ring in ones and twos and tens, ever color and ever kind, the loud song-talk of the auctioneer meeting them when they came in and following them as they went out.

After I had been watching nearly an hour and a half—plenty long enough to have seen a good show, anyway—I saw Hud walk up and slip his arm around one of the waitresses. He patted her about belly level, almost making her drop a tray of beer bottles. When she saw who it was she just laughed and slipped on by him. He spotted me and came over.

"Homer seen you?" he asked.

"Not since we got here," I said.

"He's ready for you to load them milk cows," Hud said. He pushed his straw hat off his sweaty forehead. "Good milk cows," he said. "We oughta keep 'em and let the fuckin' government go to hell. Get 'em at chute number five. I got to see a feller right quick."

I went out into the dusty heat of the parking lot, to the pickup. The door handle was so hot I had to put my gloves on to open it, and the cab was like an oven. I drove around to the loading chutes, hoping not to have to wait, but a farmer in a new International was getting him a few scrawny Brown Swiss at the chute I was supposed to use. I sat in the cab, broiling in my own juice for fifteen minutes, while he got his business done.

As soon as he left, I backed up. While I was fixing my endgates a kid a little younger than me came walking up the chute. He just looked like a city high-school kid, ducktails and flowery shirt, but he had a piece of rubber hose in his hand, like the yard men used.

"You want some cattle?" he said. "We'll load 'em for you. That's all we do, load cattle." Old Andy, the regular loader, came up right behind him, and I told them both who I was and what I was after.

"I know 'em," Andy said. "Come in here last night from Cache, Oklahoma." He slouched back down the dusty alleyway after the cows, but the kid never moved.

"I'm Marlet," he said. "I coulda gone and got 'em. I knew where they was as good as Andy." He swung the piece of water hose back and forth. "Shit," he said, "I been working in these yards ever time I get a day off, helpin' 'em load cattle. I don't care whether they pay me or not, I still come an' help."

"Damn, why?" I said. "You couldn't get me out in this heat and dust to work for nothin'."

He slapped the board fence with his hose. "I

102

don't mind it hot," he said. "We used to live on a farm an' work all the time, till Ma and Pa separated. Then we moved up here. I work for the Dr. Pepper bottlin' company ever day 'cept Sundays and Tuesdays."

"Do you have a horse?" he asked, looking at me closely out of his marbly black eyes. He asked like I was guilty of something bad. I told him I had three, all of them no-count.

"Someday I'm goin' to," he said. "I'll come over here an' chase ever one of these cattle out of the pens, ever fuckin' one. They make wienie sausage out of 'em, did you know that?"

About that time the three Jersey cows came up the chute, with Andy following them. I got behind the endgate out of sight, but Marlet stood right where he was, right in the way. He had an unlit cigarette in his mouth, and he just stood there looking at the cows. Of course they turned back down the chute, and Andy had to jump around like crazy to keep them from going by him.

"Goddamnit kid, you're in the way," Andy yelled, waving his punch pole at Marlet. The kid didn't look at Andy at all, but he climbed up on the fence, and the cows came running up the plank and into the pickup. As the last one went underneath him he reached down and hit her as hard as he could with the piece of hose.

"I like to hear it pop," he said, the cigarette still between his lips. "Did you know they make wieners out of 'em?" He sat on the fence, cooler than I was, while I fastened the endgate and hooked the chain behind it.

I had to wait for Granddad and Hud, so I pulled the pickup over in the shade of the auction barn and opened both the doors. I was going to lay down in the seat, but Marlet came and got in on the other side. He still had his hose.

"The police told me not to go with no more girls," he said. "They said they could put me in jail if I did. It's about to strangle me." He looked at me with such a serious expression on his face that I felt like I had to at least turn and face him. I really wished he would go back to the lots, so he'd be in Andy's way instead of in mine.

"I got a theory," he said. "I didn't get it from nowhere, not from no Nazis or no Communists or nobody. It says it's all right to get it. It's what God wants you to do." He leaned forward in the seat, thinking about his theory. "I'm going to make a song about it and get it on the radio," he said. "That's the way to get rich. It goes: 'It ain't no siiinn to geet iiiiit . . . !'" Then he lowered his voice. "I never got it but seven times," he said. "There used to be a whorehouse on Ohio, but the politicians closed it down for the elections." He tapped me on the knee, his eyes like black marbles. "I never got it from a blue-eyed woman once," he said. "Ever time from a brown-eyed woman. Ain't that terrible? I mean, you know?" Then he went on. "I used to go with a girl named Rosalind Chatteau, but now she won't let me go with her. I was over at my cousin's house the other day and he had three women there. They ever one had brown eyes." He looked around at the chutes, where Andy was yelling at some cattle. I thought he was going to jump out and go help, but he changed his mind. "You know what sugar dibetus is?" he asked. I nodded that I did. "I got that," he said. "There's three kinds of insulin you got to take. They get me so messed up it's about to strangle me."

He stopped talking, and we sat in the hot, noisy loading yard for about five minutes, not saying anything. He took the same unlit cigarette from his shirt pocket and put it between his lips. "Ma cleans over at the hide-an-renderin' plant," he said. "We live over there." Suddenly he got out of the cab and stood looking at the chutes, popping the water hose against his leg. "You-all have a ranch?" he asked.

When I said yes, he shook his head as if he'd known it all along. "I wish we did," he said. He took a couple of steps toward the pens, and then came back and looked up at me. "Take it easy," he said. "Or any way you can get it."

I thought he was the strangest kid I'd ever met. I sat there thinking about him and his strangling, until finally Granddad and Hud came out of the auction barn. Hud came around to the driver's side and motioned for me to scoot over. His face was wet with sweat. "Look at them shittin' Jerseys," he said. "Let's get out of this oven." I scooted over in the middle, where it was hottest, wishing the long drive home was over.

We were going right into the sun all the way. In the distance I could see the heat waves rising off the brown, burning land, and there was always a watery patch of mirage on the pavement ahead of us. With three people jammed into the cab, it was blistering; the sun was just dropping level with the windshield. The cloudless sky was still pale with heat. Granddad was inspecting the sales slip on the cows when he got in; he folded it carefully and tucked it into his billfold. His mind seemed to be on something far away.

"I wish you'd a cut loose from fifty more dollars and got tinted glass in this buggy," Hud said. "I'm fryin' in my own grease."

"Tinted glass wouldn't help," Granddad said. "Besides, I might not a had it to cut loose from."

"Oh, but you did," Hud said. "Fifty times fifty."

Granddad said nothing to that, and Hud fell silent as we drove through the big ranch country. The rush of air through the little window whipped the black locks of hair on his forehead back and forth. He nor Granddad neither one seemed in a bad arguing mood, but sitting there between them, I began to feel uncomfortable, like I was riding a horse along a high slippery ledge when it was raining. One splash of words in the wrong place and I didn't know where we'd be. For the first time, then, I noticed how much fresher and more powerful Hud looked than Granddad. Granddad was tough and steady, but he was looking awful tired and old.

"I saw you talking on the telephone for a good long while," Hud said. "Talkin' to the vet?"

"I talked to him," Granddad said. "But I didn't get a whole lot of information out of him."

"Hell, did you expect to?" Hud asked. "When a government son of a bitch wants you to know something he'll call you, or else send you a telegram."

"I reckon that's right," Granddad said. "He said they were watching the test animals pretty close, but hadn't nothin' showed up yet. I guess it'll be a few days yet before we know anything."

Hud took a toothpick out of his pocket and began to pick his teeth as he drove. I couldn't figure why he was keeping so quiet about it all, and I guess Granddad couldn't either.

"What's your idea on all this, Scott?" he asked. "What do you think we'll have to do?"

"Why I don't know nothin'," Hud said, grinning suddenly. "You're the boss, you must be the one who knows if anybody does. I just work from the shoulders down, myself." We had heard that line of talk a thousand times, and Granddad just waited it out.

"I agreed to the long quarantine," he said. "Don't you reckon that'll satisfy 'em?"

Hud spit his toothpick out the window. "Shit," he said, "they don't need you to agree to nothin'. They're the law. They'd just as soon do something you didn't agree to. You can agree with 'em till shit quits stinkin' for all the good it'll do you."

"These fellers ain't that bad," Granddad said, his eyes squinted almost shut against the direct light of the sun. "You ain't met these fellers. The boss seems to be as nice as he can be."

"I'm just here drivin'," Hud said. "Just workin' with my hands."

"Goddamnit, now, I'm asking you," Granddad said. "You been adyin' to be asked. Do you think they'd come in an' liquidate?"

Hud took his eyes off the road and looked at Granddad; he wasn't grinning any more. "Hell yes, they'll liquidate," he said. "But let me tell you something. Don't be abotherin' to ask me now. You done missed the time for that. You missed about fifteen years."

Granddad sighed. "Now what the hell do you want?" he asked. "I don't doubt I treated you hard, and I don't doubt I made some mistakes. A man don't always do what's right. But that was over an' done with years ago. It ain't got nothin' to do with this."

"You just think it ain't," Hud said. "It may be over, but it ain't done with by a long shot. Not none of it." Hud was talking slow, and watching the road, but the words he said came spurting out in the close cab like blood from a chicken's neck. "You're too old to know what I want," he said. "You always were. Not only too old, but too blind an' stingy an' contrary." Granddad listened without changing his face or saying a word. "You never thought I wanted more than you was a mind to give, did you?" Hud said. "You let that bronc fall on you an' mash you up so you thought you was goin' to die, and you got Ma to nurse you, an' she thought the same thing, an' you ended up marryin' her. Then you got well an' found out she wasn't such a bargain, and I was just part of it, just another muscle-head for you to boss around. You thought I oughta drive that goddamn feed wagon for you, instead of goin' to college. Yeah. You held on tight then, but you sure let me go in a hurry when the draft board started lookin' for somebody to go do the fightin'. But hell, you were Wild Horse Homer Bannon in them days, an' anything you did was right. I even thought you was right myself, most of the time. Why, I used to think you was a regular god. I don't no more."

Granddad seemed to have quit listening to him. "It ain't hard to look behind you an' see mistakes," he said, after a minute. "This here's a different day, an' I don't see what drivin' that feed wagon has got to do with this hoof-an'-mouth. But I guess if they try an' liquidate we can hold 'em off some way, lawyers maybe." He looked out the window.

Hud looked over at him and laughed his hard, slapping laughter. "Lawyers my ass," he said. "Fuck a bunch a lawyers. Now you asked me, I'll tell you what I'd do. I'd get on the telephone tonight and sell ever breed cow you got. They ain't got no chain on you yet, and we could ship the old bitches out before you finish them tests."

We both looked over at him like we thought he was crazy, but I knew he wasn't. He just always came out with the first scheme that popped into his head, however crazy-sounding it was.

"You mean try an' pass this shittin' stuff off on some old boy who wouldn't know what he was gettin'?" Granddad said. "I'd have to be a whole lot worse off than I am to do that."

"Hell, no," Hud said. "Sell 'em to someone stupid enough to buy 'em knowing what the situation was. There's a many of 'em dumb enough to do it, just on the gamble."

"Oh, I don't doubt there's some that would," Granddad said. "But that ain't no way to get out of a tight."

"Well, let me tell you somethin' else," Hud said. "I'll tell you what all this has got to do with the feed wagon, you don't see it yourself. Someday I'm gonna have your land, Mr. Bannon, and right here may be where I get it. You're the old senile bastard who bought them Mexico cows, and you're the one better get us out of this jam, if you don't want to end up working from the shoulders down yourself."

"I believe you're locoed," Granddad said. "What in hell do you mean?"

"Oh I ain't figured it all out perfect yet," Hud said, "but I can give you an idea. The main thing is you, old man. You're too old to cut the mustard any more. Ain't that how the song goes?" He slapped me on the leg suddenly, like we had a big secret between us. "Liquidate or not," he said. "When this is over you might as well just get you a rockin' chair, so you'll be outa my way."

Granddad looked at him like he couldn't believe his ears, and Hud pushed his hat back off his head and went on talking, the old-time wildness in his voice. "I'm gonna have this ranch a yours," he said. "Someday I am. I'm gonna give the orders on it. I ain't got it figured out perfect yet, but you can put that much down in your book right now. I may get it now, and I may have to wait a few years, but I'm gonna get it."

"How do you figure you could get it now?" Granddad said.

Hud kinda laughed. "Someway," he said. "When a man your age goes off an' buys a bunch a sick cows, it means he's too old an' daffy to operate any longer. My mamma's got an interest here that needs protectin'. You got a lot of this stuff after she married you, and some of it's hers. You got the incompetence, and hotrod here's too young to take over. Them lawyers you was atalking about might figure it so I ended up with the power of attorney. I don't know. But if I don't get it one way, I'll get it another."

"Why you're badly mistaken about all this," Granddad said. "I'll be the only one runs this ranch

111

while I'm above ground. After that you might get some of it, I don't know. But you can't get my power of attorney no way in the world."

"Pity I can't," Hud said. "You just don't make no bets on that. What I said was, I was goin' get your land."

"You ain't even consistent," Granddad said. He kept looking at Hud like he couldn't believe his ears.

"Who gives a shit," Hud said. "I'm gonna be boss." A shiny blue Cadillac passed us, and he pounded his fist against the pickup door. "Look at that blond head, would you," he said, pointing at the dressed-up woman who was driving. "How'd you like to crawl in with that?" he said, slapping my leg. Granddad frowned, and Hud laughed.

"I guess I better watch my language," he said. "I don't want to corrupt no minors." He chuckled. "But don't you know, if a man could get her in the back seat she'd make some cat tracks on that ceiling."

We drove on, forty miles an hour all the way home. Granddad and Hud got silent, both of them thinking of the times ahead, I guess. When we got to Thalia the sun was low in the west, and it was beginning to get cool. The merchants were closing up their businesses and walking home to supper. Old Man Hurshel Jones was out watering his lawn, and he waved when he saw our pickup go by. He was an old ex-cowboy who put in his days in the domino parlor; he had worked for Granddad at one time. We crossed the railroad tracks and saw the switchman's little girl out wading in a mud puddle, where the water main had leaked. "Wet plumb up to her Adam's apple," Hud said. He drove on out of town, past the junk yard, and past the cotton gin that had never ginned a bale that I could remember. The sun was a big red ball, sitting about a foot above the horizon; it wasn't hot and white any more. Hank hadn't got in yet, so we just left the milk cows in his pen and told his wife. We drove across the highway, and up the dirt road between the mesquites. When we hit the cattle guard the dogs came running out to bark at us, and wag their stub tails. No one was on the porch, but there was already a light in the living room. Halmea was in the back yard, wrestling a big rug off the clothesline.

Hud stopped the pickup by the yard fence. "I got something to do that can't wait," he said. "You-all take it from here." He walked to the fence, put one hand on a post, and jumped over.

"Oh me," Granddad said. "I wish I could move like that. I believe I'll get out too. You can take the pickup on to the barn."

He got out, and shut the pickup door carefully. Seeing Hud jump the fence reminded me of the years when he cared to be an athlete. He rodeoed a good deal, and in the summertime he caught for the local ball team. Some of the Thalia sports got enough money together to run a string of lights around the ball field, and for a few years after that, night ball games were big affairs. Hud would catch with just a mask and a glove for protection. Half the time he wouldn't even use the mask. One night he almost got his thumb torn off by a tip, but he got him a can of kerosene and soaked the thumb between innings and went on catching. He would cuss the batters till they got so mad they'd swing blind. "Stick a fork in him, he's done," he used to say.

I drove on down to the lots and put the pickup in its shed. Jesse was in the horse lot, unsaddling Granddad's young horse. He had decided to enter him in the cutting horse contest at the rodeo, just for the experience, and he was working him pretty hard. I turned on the water in the big trough, and sat on the iron edge while it filled up, sloshing my hands. I could see the round white moon reflected in the water, with little bits of green moss floating over the reflection like thunderclouds. I dipped one hand and tried to slosh out the moon, but it kept rocking back and forth. Seeing it made me think of Marcia, my cousin. When we were kids we used to float kindling ships back and forth across the tank to one another; I didn't even know what had become of Marcia. The day had left me tired in a strange way, and I was about in the mood to skip supper and lay down in the short grass and rest, lay there and watch the white moon move across the sky. I bet Marlet had never fiddled around a water tank, sailing boats with a girl like Marcia. I flipped a stick into the tank and watched it bob on the rising water. It made me think of an old hillbilly song by Moon Mulligan, called "I'll Sail My Ship Alone." With all the dreams I own. Sail it out across the ocean blue.

"Better turn that water off," Jesse said. "It's sloshin' over." He was going to supper, and I walked up to the yard with him, listening to him brag on Granddad's colt. He seemed real quiet, but friendly, and in a good mood. When we got to the gate we met Hud coming out, dressed in his rodeo clothes.

"Gimme room," he said, grinning. "I'm going up to Burk to the rodeo. You honchos wanta go?"

I was so surprised I didn't say anything, but Jesse grinned and shook his head. "No thanks for me," he said. "I'm gonna stay here and scare up a checker game."

"I guess that is about your speed," Hud said. He got into his convertible and left, with us standing there watching him.

"That's the first time in my life he ever asked me to go anywhere," I said. "I wonder why he did it."

Jesse took a package of cigarettes out of his pocket. "Lonesome, I imagine," he said. "Just tryin' to scare up a little company."

"Him lonesome?" I said. "Why he can get more women company than anybody around here."

"That ain't necessarily much," Jesse said. "It ain't necessarily company, neither. Women just like to be around something dangerous part of the time.

Scott ain't so mean but what he could get lonesome once in a while."

"You shoulda heard him this afternoon," I said. "You'd think he was mean." I sat down on the steps and began to clean my boots, and Jesse went on in to wash up for supper. When the time came, I turned out to be hungry after all.

CHAPTER

7

1.

Maybe it was Marlet, at the auction, or maybe it was Hud's wild talk on the way home, but whatever it was caused it, I had the blues that night, and everthing I did made them get worse. After supper, Halmea went to her cabin, and I wandered into the living room looking for a new magazine to read. Grandma and Granddad were there, each one sitting by a separate radio. They disagreed over the programs so much that they couldn't get along with just one. "Fibber an' Molly'll be on in a minute," Granddad said. "Sit down an' listen." The wallpaper in the room made the light seem yellow as sulphur. Granddad's face seemed thinner than it had; he hadn't shaved, and the short silver whiskers looked ragged against his skin. He wasn't being as clean about his tobacco chewing as he usually was. Neither one of them paid much attention to me, and I leaned on the mantel and read an old copy of the *Cattleman*. Grandma was listening to *Break the Bank*, and the two programs blaring so loud against each other made me want to grit my teeth. It gave me the terrible feeling that things were all out of kilter, all jumbled up. But I couldn't seem to leave them, the two old ones. I sat down by the mantel, under the picture of my folks, and read through the old magazine. I wished I could get Granddad out on the porch, into the cool night. In a minute he turned the radio dial to another station, but it turned out that Fibber and Molly had gone off the air for the summer, or maybe forever. Granddad kept fiddling with the dial, trying to find a program that suited him, and I got up and left the room, more depressed than ever.

My room didn't do much to cheer me up. I read in about half a dozen books, but I couldn't get interested in any of them, and I finally fished out a couple of old *Playboys* and went through them, looking at the shiny, naked girls. But whatever I did, that night, I just seemed to get more and more restless; it was like an itch there's no way to scratch.

Sometime late in the night I woke up, and for a minute I was all right, cool and fresh. For a while I lay on the bed enjoying the breeze, but then, when I couldn't slide back into sleep, my restlessness came back, stronger than it had been before. The longer I lay there the worse it got. The house was quiet, but I figured it must be nearly morning. I dressed and went downstairs, meaning to go out to the wind-mill. But when I was on the back porch I got another idea: I found a flashlight, a twenty-two, and a box of hollow-point shells.

I decided to go shoot things, shoot anything I could find. About halfway to the barn I stepped off the trail and walked carelessly through the high weeds, not caring how many rattlesnakes I stepped on. I was wishing I had a frog gig, I was in a mood to gig things. You gig things you got them. But I went on through the dark brush anyway. The first thing I did when I came to the tank was step on a big cottonmouth. He slid on by me to the water. I waved the flashlight around till I spotted a big bullfrog, sitting on the bank about twenty feet away. Then I sat down on the Bermuda grass, so I could hold the light on the frog and aim the gun across my knees. I hit him, heard the hollow-point splat into him, but before I could get him he flopped into the water. "Smart aleck," I said. "Now the turtles eat you." I shot five or six more frogs, some of them pretty long shots, but they all flopped into the water. Then I shot a turtle and splattered his shell. I missed a moccasin and hit a couple more frogs, and my gun was empty. I felt like shit, like all the bullets had been hitting me. I thought of Marlet, and I wished I could have shot him, the crazy little bastard. A rabbit came hopping up on the dam and I shined my light and blasted him. He kicked and died. "Tonight I may shoot everything," I said. Then I shot another big frog and got him before he flopped. I held him up by the legs and let him kick. "See what good it does you," I said. Then

I threw him out in the tank. "Feed the turtles," I said. "Frog a day keeps the doctor away." I was shaking all over, and I had frog blood on my pants leg where the big one had flopped against me. I went over and picked up the rabbit and threw him as far out in the water as I could. "Eat hearty," I said to the turtles. "I hope you get rabbit poisoning." Then I went out in the darkness, the sunflowers and milkweeds up to my chest. A sunflower scraped my wrist and I dropped the flashlight—I went on and left it shining up through the weeds. Then I went back and picked it up. Suddenly the high weeds and the darkness made me feel like Marlet, like I was strangling. "Oh me," I said. "I wasted all those frogs."

I guess the shooting woke Halmea up, because there was a light in her cabin. But before I could get there to calm her down it went out, and I went on to the house and put up the gun. I got scared and sad about what I'd done, especially about walking through all those snaky weeds. I could still hear the bullets plop into the peaceful, sleeping green frogs. The night around me was still and heavy as a blanket, and I knew I didn't want to lie down beneath it, not then. I felt like you do sometimes in a high fever, when everything goes out of focus and gets far away, and your hands feel the wrong size. I heard the little gray moths tapping against the porch screen, and I went out again. All the stars were lost in cloud. West, behind the barn somewhere, I heard the hot farting roll of thunder. The dogs had dug holes in the cool dirt where the water tank overflowed, and I stepped over them going to the windmill. I knelt by the faucet and laid my cheek against the cool iron of the water pipe. The water ran over my feet, slow at first, then coming out of the pipe in cold white spurts. I made it run slowly; on my hot back and shoulders it felt like ice. In a little while I felt too cool, and I turned it off and started to climb up to the platform. But I stopped halfway up the ladder. It was lonesome on the windmill. The rig lights were far away and dim. I thought of Halmea, of seeing her light on, and I thought how good it would be if she were still awake, so we could sit and talk awhile.

The thicket of clouds was moving westward, the moon hidden somewhere in it. It was so dark I almost stepped on an old hen that was squatting in the trail. When she squawked I jumped a foot. Then for the second night in a row I stood by Halmea's window screen and listened to her breathing. But she must not have been sleeping very soundly. When I scratched on the screen and whispered, she came right away awake.

"What you mean, nigger?" she said.

"No, it's me agin," I said. "I thought you were awake."

"Lonnie?" she said. I guess she remembered the night before. "You gettin' crazy sleepin' habits." Then she turned over on the bed and laughed so you could have heard her in Thalia. "You beats a goose," she said, laughter spilling out around the words. She sounded relieved, and I paid the laughing no mind.

"Maybe I better stay out here," I said.

"Whut fo'?" she said. "Come in here, you wants to talk so bad." I could barely make out the white of her nightgown as she got out of bed. "If it ain't dark I don' know whut it is," she said.

She shoved a chair where I could feel my way to it, then went back to the bed. "Set down," she said. "Nobody gonna swallow you." The old bedsprings squeaked when she flopped back on them. Now that I was in the room with her, I began to get nervous.

"You a crazy one," she said. She seemed tickled about something, but she changed her tune when I told her about the shooting.

"You done dat?" she said. "Dat scared de livah outa me."

"I don't know why I did it," I said. "I didn't have nothin' else to do, for one thing."

"Sheew," she said, "dat's no reason. You had de blues about sometin', I seen dat at suppah."

"I'm just sick of all this," I said.

Suddenly she clicked on the little lightbulb at the head of her bed, and the yellow light spread over the room, as welcome as the sun. "Sick uv whut, honey?" she said. "Tell me little more." She looked at me out of her calm black eyes, smiling the least little bit. I got tight and embarrassed when I saw her, I couldn't help it. Her breasts sagged heavy against the nightgown, her bare legs tucked up under her as she watched me.

"Things used to be better around here," I said. "I feel like I want something back."

"Pity," she said. She picked up her pillow and held it in her lap. "You mighty young to be wantin' things back," she said.

"If Granddad and Hud could get along a little better it would be okay," I said.

She grinned a little, and then a solemn look came on her face. "If an' if an' if," she said. "You if youself crazy. I been ifin' aroun' lot longah dan you have, an' whut it get me? Just whut I eats an' whut I wears out."

We sat quiet for a minute; Halmea had a faraway, solemn look on her face. Her lips were puffed a little. "Ain't much talk, is it?" she said, and I nodded. Outside, the chickens were squawking, and the chicken house was a shadow in the first gray light. Halmea was picking the flaky brown paint off the bedrail, pursing her lips like she wanted to whistle. It was peaceful and nice for a while: I had quit thinking about anything. She clicked off the lightbulb, and we sat in the dim gray room.

"I just work while I ifs," she said. "When I get dat done I works a little mo'." She stood up, yawned and stretched her back. "My back gonna quit me first," she said. "Den I guess I just if." She went to the screen door and looked out into the grayness. "Cloudy," she said. "Now you get on.

You got mo' kinks in you dan I got in my back." She stood in the doorway, scratching one leg through the white gown, while I walked up the path in the cool of morning. She would be going to the house, to cook breakfast, but I knew it was almost an hour away, so instead of going up to my room I went quickly to the lots and took my bridle from a nail in the harness shed. Then I went to the oatbin and scooped some yellow oats in a bucket. I took the oats and the bridle and walked back through the dewy grass toward the tank, hoping to meet the horses on the way.

2.

They weren't at the tank, but I stood on the dam and watched them coming out of the brush to the north, trailing to the lots for their morning feed. The fish were making dawn breathrings on the gray sheet of the water. When the horses got close enough I shook the oat bucket at them, and they filed over to me one by one. Each one stretched his neck and took a mouthful, afraid of being caught. When Stranger came up I set the bucket on the ground and let him nose it; while his head was down I slipped the reins around his neck. I bridled him, and poured the rest of the oats in little piles for the other horses. A covey of bobwhites whistled behind the dam; I waited a minute and saw them trail down to water. I hung the empty oat bucket on a snag.

Stranger let me slip on his bare back, and we trotted off toward our big valley pasture. When I got through the gate, the dewy grass stretched away in front of me, almost six miles to another fence. The dawn breeze stirred in my face: the sky to the east was brightening. Idiot Ridge was a mile away, breaking the levelness of the plain. I touched Stranger into a steady lope, so we could get there and wait for the sun. Dozens of feeding jack rabbits broke before us, but as we went past they zigzagged off to the side and stopped, their long ears folded against their heads. A big, brown-winged prairie hawk sat on the limb of a dead mesquite, watching for quail. Once Stranger jumped a small mesquite bush when I wasn't looking, and I almost slid off his slick back. When we got to the ridge I slowed him down, and he picked his way through the loose gray rocks to the top.

On the north edge of Idiot Ridge I stopped and slid off. Headquarters lay to the northeast, where the sun was about to come up. The whole long line of sky behind the house and barn was orange and red; the wind was driving the layer of summer clouds out of sight to the northwest. I could see the horses we had left at the tank, filing up to the lots for their regular feed. In a few minutes Jesse would tend to them. Farther down the ridge two hawks were gliding low over the rocky hillside, dipping and swooping, then almost steady in the air. Stranger whinnied, then bent his neck and began to graze. The sky was a country of changing colors, like the land: red in the east, still deep night blue in the west. The moon was fading out of sight. Across the thread of highway, in a neighbor's pasture, an old bull bellowed, the hoarse sound barely reaching me. I could see a few of Granddad's cows on the flats to the south. Suddenly Stranger raised his head and snorted. Two young dog coyotes were trotting along the edge of the ridge, coming right toward us. When they were about fifty yards away, I whistled and they stopped, their gray heads cocked and alert. Then they loped off the slope over the edge and I lost them among the rocks and chaparral. Fingers of sunlight crept up the ridge, crept over us, and made Stranger's sorrel coat shine like fire. I watched the light brighten the rangeland a minute; then I got back on and touched Stranger with my heels. I turned him directly toward the barn, so I wouldn't have to stop and open the horse pasture gate. Sliding off the steep ledges I was afraid to give him much slack, but once we hit bottom, with only level pastureland between us and the homeplace, I let him go. In a hundred yards he went from trot to lope to dead, tearing run, till he was stretched out low to the ground, with his red legs blurred beneath him. I couldn't see for the wind tears in my eyes, and I was afraid every second I would fall off, but I let him go. It seemed like I had been waiting a week for the thrill and excitement of his speed. We went over the gray-brown grass like it was a race track, Stranger running for all he was worth and me leaning over his neck hanging on to his flying mane.

Suddenly, out of the corner of my eye, I saw a fence and knew we were nearly there and must stop. It was the fence that led to the lots, I remembered that the lot cornered, that Stranger would whip around it, and I started to slow him down. But it was too late, he was turning without me, slipping away from between my legs, already turned and gone, the reins burning through my hands, the ground somewhere below or behind me. Then I hit it, I was rolling, a rock bumped my hip, there was nothing to grab, then no more rolling and I sat up, wondering if I were hurt. Suddenly Jesse had ahold of my shoulders and was trying to push me back down. "Be still," he said. "Be still. You may have something broken." But I wanted to stand up, I felt too good to be still.

"I'm okay," I said. His face was pained, like he was the one who was hurt. It must have been a terrible fall to watch. Stranger stood by the lot gate, the bridle reins trailing in the dirt. I grinned, and Jesse's face relaxed a little. He gripped me under the arms and helped me up.

"It looked like both your legs would break off," he said.

My hip was sore from the rock, but otherwise I didn't seem to have a scratch on me. I led Stranger through the gate and slipped the bridle off as he went by me to the hayrack.

"He runs like an antelope," Jesse said. "All the years I followed rodeo I never seen a harder-lookin' fall."

"It wasn't as hard as it looked," I said. Walking to the house for breakfast, I felt as good as I had in weeks. I was even hoping there was a day's work ahead.

3.

By the time I had finished my Post Toasties, everybody else was nearly done eating. Hud had his mouth full of biscuit, and was pouring a dark stream of sorghum over a lump of butter that lay in his plate. He had on slacks and a white shirt, dressed up to go somewhere. Granddad was saucering his coffee, not paying much attention to the breakfast-table conversation. When breakfast was over he got his hat and went out the back door. I ate as quickly as I could and started to the lots, but Halmea stopped me.

"You in no hurry," she said. "Help me strain dis milk."

The two big buckets of milk Lonzo had brought up stood on the back porch; the yellow layer of cream had already risen to the top. Halmea handed me a piece of cheesecloth, and I spread it over the top of the old milk strainer. She lifted one of the heavy buckets and slowly poured the milk through the cloth into the clean straining basin. The milk ran through in a swirling white stream, leaving the little flecks of dirt and manure stuck to the damp cheesecloth. Clear beads of sweat stood on the black dark skin of Halmea's throat and neck.

"Watch what you doin'," she said. "You let dat rag slip an' we got it all to do ovah."

When we were finished I got my hat and went down to the lots, to see what the day's assignment was. Granddad was in the tool shed, sharpening the blade of his shovel.

"What do we do today?" I asked. "I feel almost like workin' for a change."

"Goodness, I wish I had a job for you," he said, cleaning the file against his pants leg. He put his weight on the shovel handle, to hold the blade steady against the bench, and sharpened a little while he was considering.

"Oh, son, I wasn't gonna do much today," he said. "I'm just gonna cut a few weeds here around the house. I guess this mornin' you better go with the boys and help 'em patch some of that fence on the west side. I don't guess we'll do much this afternoon. Kinda hate to waste work until I find out a little more about the cattle." The rasp of the file drowned out conversation for a minute, and I stood there watching. Seeing him sweat over the shovel, I wished I could stay and cut weeds with him. I didn't feel right about leaving him to work alone.

"You ain't worried about that scheme of Hud's, are you?" I asked. He laid the file down and tested the edge of the blade with his finger.

"Hud?" he said. "What scheme? Oh lordy, I got so many things lined up to worry about I ain't come to that. I imagine Scott was talkin' not too serious. I don't think he's got much of a scheme in his mind."

He shook his head and picked up the file. "If I don't get a bill of health on these cattle there won't be much ranch for him to run," he said.

"Aw, I don't really think they'll liquidate these cattle," he said, after he had filed a minute. "But I ain't young enough to count on what I think bein' right, either, an' I ain't fool enough to figure on things turning out the way I expect 'em to." He put up the file and started off around the barn. Jesse hollered at me then, and I went over to the post pile and helped him and Lonzo load the fencing tools.

4.

None of us worked very hard that morning. There didn't seem to be any reason to strain ourselves. By eleven-thirty we were sitting on the back porch, waiting for Halmea to call dinner. While we were waiting, Lonzo and Jesse got to talking about the towns they knew. Lonzo's travels didn't take long to tell—after he named the times he'd got drunk in Lawton or Ardmore or Oklahoma City, he was about through. But Jesse could have talked all afternoon and on into the night and not have scratched the surface of all the things he'd seen and done. He got to talking about places he'd been on the rodeo circuit, and just hearing the names was enough to make me restless. He'd been to practically ever town in Texas, big or little, Lubbock and Amarillo and Houston, Fort Worth and Dallas and

San Antone, Alpine and El Paso, Snyder and Olney,
Vernon and Dumas and Newcastle and a hundred
more, and then on into New Mexico and Colorado,
to Tucumcari and Clovis and Gallup and Cimarron, Raton and Walsenburg and Denver, on up to
Cheyenne and Pendleton and Pierre and Calgary,
over to St. Louis and Sioux City, Chicago and
Kansas City and New York, and a hundred more I
couldn't even remember. I could tell by the way he
rolled the names around in his mouth that he must
have liked rodeo, or at least have liked seeing
places. But he wouldn't admit it.

"That's no life," he said. "You boys think stayin'
in one place is tiresome, just wait till you see that
goddamn road comin' at you ever mornin'. And
still comin' late that evenin' and sometimes way
into the night. I run that road for ten years and
never caught up with nothin'."

"I'd like to run that bastard," Lonzo said. "Long
as I could chase down a piece of pussy now and
then, to keep me goin'."

"If you stayed on it that long, you must a liked
it?" I said. He shook his head and spit.

"Oh, it gets in your blood like anything else you
do," he said. "For a while it's right excitin'." He
fanned a fly away from his face. "I just wonder,
when it's all said and done," he went on, "who ends
up with the most in this scramble. Them that go in
for big shows and big prizes and end up takin' a
bustin', or them that plug along at what they can

kinda handle. Home folks or show people. They's a lot a difference in 'em."

"Which are you?" I said.

"I kinda split the difference," he said. "I missed out on the good things a both kinds, loose-horsing like I have." The way he said it, I couldn't help noticing how sorry he felt for himself. "I still got some loose horse in me," he said.

Halmea called us then, and we went in and ate. After dinner, while everyone was heading for their napping spot, I went out in the front yard and set down under the cedars. I leaned back against one and let the hot wind blow in my face. Sticky cedar sap was oozing out of the trees, and I caught the burning summery smell of the lilac bushes. I thought about all those rich names Jesse had rolled off his tongue, and about what little I had to compare with them myself. Except for trips to the county-line beer joints, those few nights in Fort Worth were all I had. I guess they just amounted to a few evening walks downtown, when the city lights were flashing. But they had seemed like something rich to me. I had left Granddad in the hotel lobby, and prowled through the drugstores for a while, spinning rack after rack of shiny-covered paperbacks, and listening to jukebox music. Gradually I would work my way south, to the beery end of Main Street, where all the weirdos walked around. Old hobos would zigzag along the sidewalk, carrying bottles of wine in brown paper sacks, or else they stood under the yellow lightbulbs of the Penny Arcade, waiting for the rowdies inside to flip out cigarette butts. In the shooting galleries the tough sharpshooters with tattoos and ducktails shot the quiet white ducks that went around and around through years of bullets. Once in a while some ace would hit the bell above the ducks, and a loud *piiinng!* rang out, mixing with the honking and the talk. About every two doors there would be a bar, dim and dark inside, but pouring loud talk and hillbilly guitar music out on the sidewalks of the town. I walked in one once where three hillbilly musicians in straw hats were standing behind the bar making music for everyone. The guitar player was picking as loud and fast as he could, till finally the bar girls and drillers and truck drivers and wild cowboys, and all the men and women beering and loving in the cool, dim leathery booths turned their heads to listen and clap. Everybody went to laughing and yelling and slapping down silver on the tables, and on the dance floor the dancers hugged and whirled in the blue darkness and the smoke. The only ones who weren't having a good time were a few lonesome-looking boys at the bar. When the musicians went off to drink beer, the jukebox flared up and played hillbilly dance music the rest of the time I stayed. It played old songs by Hank Williams and Ernest Tubb and Kitty Wells, and it was cold, cold hearts in the darkness, with dancers bumping into each other and going on to dance some more.

Those that didn't dance sat in the booths and drank from the sweaty bottles of beer. It was no more work and no more lonesome, and all the honky-tonk angels living it up. I slipped out and went on past a few more bars, and past the mission and the shouting preachers, and past the pawnshops with their windows full of switchblades and guitars, all the way down to the Mexican picture show. Next to it was a tattoo parlor where I saw a soldier getting a big blue eye tattooed right in the middle of his forehead. By the time I felt ready to start back to the hotel, it was late, and the street wasn't so friendly. The colored men would whisper to me from the steps of the run-down hotels, whispering about women upstairs. Some of the hobos I had seen on my way from the hotel would be sitting spraddle-legged against the buildings, coughing. The lonesome boys that had been in the bars would be leaning on telephone poles or standing by their cars, no one to go to and no one coming along. The bars were quieter, but the same sad music, Kitty and Hank and Ernest, reached out of the doors to pull the boys back in. I saw a few fights, saw cops running into bars, once saw blood on the sandy sidewalk, where a boy had been stabbed. But I even enjoyed the shatter of those nights: things were moving around me, and it was exciting. One night a blonde girl in a pink rodeo hat ran by me and jumped in an Oldsmobile convertible, but her boy friend jumped in and grabbed her before she could get away. He jerked her hand off the ignition and shook her till her hat fell off and her white blond hair was tossed and tangled. "I'll coldcock you, you're just beggin' me to," he said. "Carl, don't, gimme my purse," she said, and he shook her some more. "I'll stomp that bastard's ass," he said. I walked away, back toward the hotel. That same night a crowd of rich city kids came out of a fancy eating place and laughed at me. The boys had flowers on their white coats, and the girls wore long lacy evening gowns. "Cowboys are darlin'," one girl said. That's all right, I thought. They were too silly even to bother giving them the finger. I went on to my room and went to bed. When I turned over I could see the city lights, still red and green and yellow, blinking through the blind; and later, after I had slept awhile, I heard the far-off sound of an ambulance screaming through old Cowtown's morning streets.

It wasn't like what all Jesse had seen, but it was something. I raised up on one elbow under the cedars and looked over the pastures south, toward Fort Worth. Heat waves rose off the land, so that the cars on the highway were blurred. A loose wire was rattling on the yard fence. The front door slammed, and Granddad came out to empty his tobacco can. When he went back in the house he held on to the porch pillar a minute, to steady himself. I got up and brushed the dirt and the cedar needles off my pants. I was thinking that some night I would talk Granddad out of the Lincoln, and Hermy and I and a few other boys could take a quick trip to Fort Worth. If we left early we could make it down there by nine or ten o'clock, and be back by sunup. That would leave plenty of time to do more than we had ever done.

CHAPTER

8

1.

The rodeo people began to move into Thalia the day before the show actually began. That day they brought in the rodeo stock, and the contestants came to town, some of them off the circuit, and some just off the ranches. The poor boys came with nothing but their rigging and a change of clothes, but the winners drove in in big white Lincolns, with fancy horse trailers hitched on behind. The cowgirls came too, wearing big hats, and britches that fitted them like skin fits a snake. I don't guess they ever slept from the time they hit town until the rodeo was over four days later. During all that time there was nothing but beer drinking and rodeo talk, courting and dancing, and even the merchants in Thalia came out in Western wear. Rodeo was the one big get-together of the year.

Since it all came like Christmas, only once a year,

I was careful not to let any of it pass me by. The morning of the day before the show I got up before anyone and slipped out of the house and took off for town in the pickup.

I didn't eat any breakfast, so my first stop was Bill's Café. When I got there the place was already full; there were twenty or thirty cars parked out front and more driving up all the time. People were milling around like cattle in a pen. The sun was starting its long climb, the gold rays flashing on the shiny chrome of the cars. From across the highway there was the wet grassy smell of the pastures that surrounded the town. Cowboys in Stetsons and sleeveless shirts were coming out of the café, and others just like them were crowding in. I wandered around among the cars for a while, thrilled with the sound and the people and the cool morning. I walked by a muddy pink Oldsmobile, '50 model, and saw a girl I knew sprawled like a doll in the back seat. Her long black hair hid her face, and she still had a can of beer in one hand. She heard my feet on the gravel and raised up, her gray eyes blank. "Sugah?" she said. "Why dint you take me in?" She didn't recognize me, but I opened the door and sat down by her a minute. "Throw this out," she said, handing me the beer can. "I'm full." Her name was Irene. She slumped against me and went back to sleep, and I eased her down in the seat and got out. I could hear music from the café, high, loud jukebox music, and I wanted to go inside.

I was lucky to get a seat at the counter. All the

booths were full and running over. Everybody was finding friends they hadn't seen for years, or running into people they had seen the night before, and whichever it was, they sat down and talked old times. There were a few thin cowboys at the counter who didn't look so happy; they reminded me of Jesse, or the lonesome boys in the Fort Worth bars; none of it was very exciting to them. I ordered coffee and eggs, and sat there swinging back and forth on my red-topped stool, listening to the music and the roar. Ever time I swung I saw my reflection on the shiny milk machine; my cowlick was sticking up, and I knew if Hermy had seen it he would have kidded me and sung about Jennie, with the light brown hair like mine. The big jukebox was never quiet, the voices of Slim and Roy and Kitty and Ernest and Hank helping the cowboys grieve or celebrate. The waitresses in clean morning uniforms wove through the tables with gallons of coffee and big platters of eggs. The cowboys in the booths talked the sleep and the beer out of their voices, telling each other about the ride or the women or the long year's work just done. They laughed and whittled toothpicks out of matches. One cowboy with a little too much spirit had brought his rope in with him, but when he started to make a loop his buddies swarmed over him and got it away from him before he could do any damage. When they carried him out he was laughing so hard at himself that he couldn't see. I wished it was rodeo more often, so there'd be more wild breakfasts and strange crowds. I fiddled with my eggs to make it last. A cowboy near me picked his girl up and carried her outside; she laughed and kicked so much her blue shirttail came out of her rodeo pants. When I got outside he was trying to stuff her through the window of his Mercury, and a lot of other fellows were standing around giving him advice and encouragement. He got her in and stood there laughing about it, his hands in his pockets. Then she rolled up the car windows right quick and locked him out.

I went on down to the rodeo arena, to watch them unload the bulls and the bucking stock, but I was a little late. By the time I got there the old humpbacked bulls were standing by the hayracks, pulling out long strands of prairie hay. There were a couple of young guys in rodeo clothes sitting on the fence watching the bulls. I climbed up by them and made their acquaintance. They had come from Cimarron, New Mexico, to ride the bulls.

"Shit, we can't ride no closer to home," one of them said. "If my old man found out my ass would be mud."

The one that said that was a quiet-looking kid. He didn't look much like a bull rider. The other one's name was Sandefer, and he pretty well thought he was it.

"Wait till I get on one of them big bastards," he said. "The fur's gonna fly."

"Whose fur?" the other one said. He didn't really look too thrilled at the prospect of getting on one of

the old surlies, and I didn't blame him. Sandefer
popped him on the arm to cheer him up. To the
right of us, across the arena, the concession people
were moving in their popcorn machines and Sno-
Cone stands. Some carpenters were hammering
behind the chutes; a couple of bulls had got to
fighting and torn the gate down. The old gray and
black bulls looked lazy and tame as milk cows out
there eating hay, but they wouldn't look so gentle
when you got 'em crowded into a chute.

I liked to watch the bulls, but I got pretty tired of
Sandefer talking like he was Jim Shoulders or
Casey Tibbs. I left them on the fence, speculating
about which bulls they would draw. There weren't
very many people around the arena, and I went to
the grandstand and climbed up to the top seats and
sat down to watch. I could see beyond the rodeo
pens and watch half of Thalia waking up. I saw a
woman stagger out to her clothesline in a bathrobe,
to hang out an early washing. In the arena below me
a cowgirl was loping her paint horse around and
around in circles—she acted like it was the only
thing she knew how to do. The sun was getting high
enough to make my seat uncomfortable, and I got
up to go. Even in the mornings I was restless. Below
me, in the parking lot a cowboy was trying to get his
girl to come through in broad daylight. But she
wouldn't. She nearly would, but she wouldn't. Kids
were coming down the road to watch the men and
horses; they always swarmed around the rodeo
people like flies, trying to find someone who would

let them ride a horse. I watched the cowboy in the Chevy awhile, and then went down and bought me a plain Sno-Cone before I went back to the ranch.

2.

"Telephone's ringin'," Willie said. "Mistah Hack." We had just finished dinner, and were sitting around the table drinking the last cool swallows of ice tea and listening to the radio. Granddad smiled when he heard Willie come on the air.

"Hack-berry Ho-tel," Willie said. "Willie speakin'."

"Dat niggah," Halmea said.

"It's just a program," I said. "How do you know he ain't a white man?"

"Hell," Hud said, "a white man don't sound that worthless." He was sitting on the wood box picking his teeth. "Turn it over to Fort Worth and get the cattle market."

"Too late," Granddad said. "Nothin' left but the cotton quotations by now."

"That's all right," Hud said. "I'd just as soon hear cotton markets as listen to a nigger jabber. I might go into the cotton business one a these days." He stretched his arms and got up to go to the bathroom. While the program was going on we heard a car rattle the cattle guard and come around to the back of the house. I went to the back door to see who it was.

"It's Mr. Burris," I said.

"Have him come in," Granddad said.

Mr. Burris came to the back door, and I held it open for him. "You missed dinner," I said. "Your timin's off." He nodded and grinned at me, but it was easy to see he was under pretty much of a strain. He didn't walk as light and reckless as he had that first morning. When he got to the dining room he had to go through a little routine with Granddad: Mr. Burris saying he'd had plenty to eat, and Granddad trying to feed him anyway. Hud came in and Granddad introduced him. He said howdy, but he gave Mr. Burris a pretty hard looking over.

"Well, if you won't eat, we may as well move out on the porch," Granddad said. "I believe it's a little cooler out there. I guess you got something to tell us or you wouldn't be here."

Mr. Burris rubbed the back of his head and managed not to say anything. Lonzo slipped off by himself, out the back door, but the rest of us filed out and arranged ourselves on the shady porch. Granddad made Mr. Burris take the rocking chair. We all sat and chewed toothpicks awhile before anything was said.

"Well, I guess the tests are done," Granddad said, finally. He fished in his Levis for his pocket-knife.

"No, sir, actually they aren't," the vet said. "Not completely. It will be at least one more day before we can say for sure what your cattle have got. But we've got a pretty good indication now, and the way things were looking, I thought I ought to run out and talk to you. There hasn't been a sign of sickness in the horses and swine we vaccinated, but a couple of the cattle have already developed blisters. I'm afraid it's going to mean that you've got the worst thing you could have."

Granddad shook his head, and winced a little. He reached out and cut a twig off one of Grandma's hedges, and began to trim it with his knife. "I guess I mighta knowed that," he said. "I guess it didn't make sense to me how a herd of cattle could look as good as mine does and still be half dead."

"I know it's strange," the vet said. "But your cattle aren't half dead, you see. Even if the disease hit ever animal you've got it might not kill over thirty per cent, but the thing is, it might get out and kill thirty per cent of the cattle in the whole area. And the ones it didn't kill wouldn't be worth keeping." He stopped and looked out over the pastures. Hud was watching him, the match still in his mouth.

"And there's no cure atall?" Granddad said.

"None we know of," Mr. Burris said. "It's like a bolt of lightning. It don't hurt you till it hits, but then it hurts a lot."

"Oh me," Granddad said. "I was hopin' it wouldn't come to this. And you don't think there's much chance of anything changing the picture?"

"Very little," the vet said. "I'm afraid it's all but settled now. Technically, we have to wait another day, but I can't offer you any hope."

"Then it's like I said before," Granddad went on. "I'll try an' cooperate with you any way I can, short of killin' my cattle. Just anything. You let me know, and I'll do my best to get it done. If you got any new vaccines you ain't tried out, you're welcome to use these cattle to experiment on, even if it kills ever one of 'em. That way you got a chance a doin' some good. But just drivin' 'em in a pit an' shootin' 'em I can't abide that."

"I know it's a terrible thing," Mr. Burris said, facing Granddad. "Even to think about."

"Yes, it is," Granddad said. "I imagine thinkin' about it's all you ever done, ain't it? Well, sir, I've seen some of it first hand, durin' the depression, an' it's a sight worse to see than it is to think about." Granddad looked small and grizzled and determined, but his voice wasn't as final-sounding as it usually was. He sounded a little old and shaky.

Mr. Burris waited politely till he was through, and then he went right on with what he was saying. Hud watched him, but he never opened his mouth. "I'm sure you're right about that," Mr. Burris said. "I'm sure it is worse to see. But, Mr. Bannon, none of that changes the situation. You got to act how the situation lets you, and in this case you and I are both helpless so far as doing what we'd like to do is concerned."

"Maybe so," Granddad said. "I know there's a lot a times when a man is helpless—I've been in plenty of 'em. But a man's got to go on and do what he can, that's the only way he's got a finding out whether he's helpless or not. In this case I ain't convinced I am. I got a lawyer lookin' into the legal side of this, and he may turn out to know a thing or two you an' I don't."

Mr. Burris was quiet a minute. "I'm afraid you'll be disappointed if you expect much help from the law," he said. "Of course you were right to go see about it. But the law on this has already been argued a good many times, and unless it's something pretty recent that I don't know about, the lawyer will just have to tell you what I'm telling you now. The only thing you can do is liquidate."

"I can't have that," Granddad said. I looked at Hud and noticed a kinda tight grin stretching his mouth. What he was thinking was beyond me to guess.

"But, Mr. Bannon," the vet said, "you may *have* to have it. Your cattle are public enemies now. Bad enough for you to lose your herd, that I'll grant. You'll be paid a top price for every animal killed, you know that. I imagine it will be something like $300 or $350 a pair. But whatever it is it won't pay you for all the years it took you to breed these animals and get them as good as they are—we both know that. But better you lose them, breed or no breed and pay or no pay, than to have this thing spread and eventually have to kill 75,000 cattle, like they did the last time it got out. It could sure happen, and it probably will unless we handle this thing quick; it probably will."

After that, the conversation died down for a

while. Granddad sat hunched over, like he was straining to get something out. The rest of us were just waiting. Granddad looked up, and let his eyes play over the hot noontime pastures, the gray grasslands stretching before him to the east. Finally Mr. Burris decided to try another tack.

"But at least you will be paid good money," he said. "I mentioned that. And after all, Mr. Bannon, you're getting up in years. You can afford to slow down for a year—that's the period of quarantine." Granddad looked up, a little surprised, but Mr. Burris went on. He was trying hard. "Rest won't hurt your grass," he said. "It'll be just that much better for the herd you or these young men put on it. While it's empty you might sell a few oil leases or something. A ranch is more than just the cattle that's on it."

He should have kept quiet, but he didn't know. Granddad leaned back and closed his pocketknife. "Oil," he said, looking down at his hands. "Maybe I could get some, but I don't believe I will. If there's oil down there these boys can get it sucked up after I'm under there with it. Something about this sickness, maybe I can't do much about, but the oil-field stuff I can. I don't like it an' I don't aim to have it. I guess I'm a queer, contrary old bastard, but there'll be no holes punched in this land while I'm here. They ain't gonna come in an' grade no roads, so the wind can blow me away." He looked up again, across the land. "What good's oil to me," he said. "What can I do with it? With a bunch a fuckin' oil wells. I can't ride out ever day an' prowl amongst 'em, like I can my cattle. I can't breed 'em or tend 'em or rope 'em or chase 'em or nothin'. I can't feel a smidgen a pride in 'em, cause they ain't none a my doin'. Money, yes. Piss on that kinda money. I used to think it was all I was after, but I changed my mind. If I'd been in this business just for the money I'd a quit an' started sellin' pencils or something back before you were born. I still like money as well as any man, nearly, and I done with it an' without it as much an' more than most people have, and I don't ever intend to let on I don't want a big share of it. But I want mine to come from something that keeps a man doing for himself."

He stopped, and Mr. Burris sat quietly, looking helpless and nervous. There wasn't much more he could say.

"We're much obliged to you for comin' out an' tellin' us how the tests were goin'," Granddad said. "I wish they were goin' different, but I don't think we'll quit hopin' just yet. Maybe when we get the final word we can get together an' do what's right."

"I'm sure we can," Mr. Burris said, standing up. Granddad walked around to his car with him, and they talked a little more. I stayed with Jesse. Hud disappeared into the house without once opening his mouth.

"Don't sound good," Jesse said. "That talk about lawyers, I guess that's just bluff." We sat on the porch, waiting for orders, but we didn't get any.

When Hud came out again he went straight to his car.

"See you rannies," he said. "Don't get sores on your butts."

"Where that feller's going, nobody knows," Jesse said.

CHAPTER

———— 9 ————

1.

The next day Granddad went to Wichita, I guess to see his lawyers. Lonzo took a notion to enter the saddle-bronc riding contest and hitchhiked into Thalia to sign up. He had an old car, but nine tenths of the time it didn't run. Hud hadn't come in the night before, and nobody had any idea where he was. It looked like such a dull day that I went into town about nine in the morning and shot pool till dinner. The whole town had a rodeo look already, paper cups and beer cans everywhere, and piles of horseshit drying in the street. I shot bank shots until I got tired of leaning over, and then went home to dinner.

The minute we got through eating, Halmea was on Jesse and me to play checkers. She looked kinda worn down, but she claimed to be dying for a game. Jesse kept talking about how he hadn't played in thirty years, but since it was just Chinese checkers, she talked him into coming along.

"Dat's all right," she said. "I always does de best after I lays off a little while."

"Thirty years is a bare bit more than a little while," he said.

We went into her room and she pitched her stack of movie magazines off the card table onto the bed. She had a variety-store picture of Lana Turner on her dresser, and an old lumber-yard calendar with a picture of Jesus holding a lamb, hung on the wall. It was two years old.

"I'll just kick off dese floppy shoes," she said. She shoved them under the bed with her bare feet. We scooted the card table in front of the window, so it would catch what breeze there was.

"Your calendar don't keep very good time," I said.

"It do very well fo' me," she said. "It just runs a day a two off." She got out the Chinese checkerboard and laid it on the old green table. I dropped the marbles in their slots. We decided to play two at a time instead of three, and Jesse elected to watch the first game. He tilted his chair back against the wall. I began to jump Halmea's marbles right and left.

"Hellation," she said. "You movin' too fast."

"I never played that kind," Jesse said. "I used to play the other kind a good deal, when Granddad was still alive. I remember once we lived outside of

Mineral Wells, down close to the Brazos River. It was a wet winter, and all us kids had to stay inside a lot. I did more checker playing that winter than all the rest of my life put together. Anyhow, it kept Granddad in a good humor, the pore old soul."

I was moving into Halmea's triangle with my marbles, in spite of all she could do. She sighed. "I guess I had a grandpappy somewher'," she said. "But I may not, I don't know."

"I remember mine well," Jesse said. "He got killed that same winter." I was about as interested in Jesse's talk as I was in the checker game, but it didn't take much concentration to beat Halmea. "We were eatin' breakfast one mornin'," he said, "and Grandpa wasn't around. He was always getting up early and going down to a little grocery store, on the highway, right by the river, and we didn't pay it no mind if he was gone a few minutes. It was a cold, foggy river that morning, and I was on the side a the table away from the fire, about to freeze. Then a feller that worked in the store came running in and took Pa outside and told him Grandpa was dead, down on the highway. That Brazos River fog was pretty thick, and he was walkin' along too close to the pavement, and some feller from Arkansas came along in a Chevrolet and hit him without ever seein' him. Knocked him about a hundred feet off the road, and 'bout drove the man who was drivin' crazy. That was about the time Pa moved us to Lamesa, just before my oldest bud left home."

Halmea shook her head and twisted her feet around the chair legs. "Sheew," she said. "White folks families beats me. I 'member seein' my own pappy just six, seven times. Dey no tellin' where dat man is now. He may be dead as you grandpappy."

"Don't you keep up?" Jesse said.

"How you gonna keep up?" she said. "A gal can't tag him aroun'."

And they went on that way, talking back and forth, while I beat Halmea four or five times. After a while they got on the differences between white folks parties and colored folks parties, and Halmea got tickled remembering all the funny things she'd seen, till she couldn't hold the marbles for giggling and laughing about them. The marbles began to pop off and roll around on the floor, and she kept on laughing, and so finally Jesse had to take her place. He wasn't as bad about laughing, but he was more interested in the talk than in the checker playing, so when it was all over, about three o'clock, I was the undisputed Chinese-checker champion of the ranch. Halmea and Jesse were in about the best mood of their lives, and all the chuckling and fine friendly talk and the games I won made me feel good too. Finally Halmea had to go hang out a washing, and I went to the house and flopped on the living room couch, feeling loose and lazy. I felt good about Halmea and Jesse, and I dozed off to sleep.

2.

About four-thirty or five that afternoon, Halmea woke me up to tell me she was going off to a fish fry with some colored boy. I said okay, and thought no more about it. She said our supper was in the stove. Then about six-thirty, when I was dressing to go to the rodeo, Hud came home. Granddad was still gone, and I couldn't leave till he came home. Jesse had taken the colt into town in the pickup, and I would have to use the Lincoln. I was in the down-stairs bathroom when I heard a car door slam, and I thought it might be Granddad. But when I opened the bathroom door and heard all the slamming and banging in the kitchen, I knew it must be Hud, and nobody else.

When I went in he was yanking out the kitchen drawers, and pawing in the breadbox. His shirt was open all the way down his stomach, and he looked like he hadn't shaved in a week. A bottle of Hiram Walker sat on the kitchen table; it was better than two-thirds empty. Hud looked about the meanest I'd ever seen him, his hair all tangled, and his face tight and wild. It scared me a little, just seeing him.

"Where's that nigger?" he said. "I want supper an' I don't want no hesitatin' about it."

"She went to a fish fry," I said. "The supper's in the stove."

"Well, if that ain't a fragrant pile of shit," he said. "A fine bunch around here. Payin' her money to run off to a fish fry when I'm starvin' to death. I'd like to get ahold a that bitch." Granny must have heard him all the way to her room, because she came hobbling in. She looked pretty scared herself.

"There's plenty here," she said. "I'll fix you some. You sit down."

"Screw it," he said. "Sit down yourself. When I come in from a trip I want my meal on the table, not waitin' to be fixed. If this ain't a home-comin'."

"Where all did you go?" she asked.

"What's it to you?" he said, picking up his whiskey bottle. "Wait an' be surprised like the rest of 'em."

He was too wild-acting to fool with, and we both shut up. He was shifting back and forth on his feet, like a bull that had been crowded too close. "Well, get it on the table," he said. Granny began to jump around like she was twenty-five years old, and I left them and went out on the porch. I wanted to go to town, but I didn't have a way to leave. I stood on the porch and watched the cars go flashing across the land. I was wishing I had one. Then there were steps in the living room behind me, and Hud came out. "She's got tea to make yet," he said, sitting down on the steps. He had his whiskey bottle.

"Gettin' dark," he said. His voice was a little looser, but still mean. "I'll tell you, I like lots of light. I was over there in the jungle and had to lay out one night by myself, dark as hell and Japs all around me. Ever since then it's been piss on the dark."

"I got a deal goin'," he said. "It's gonna knock some people on their asses, an' you might be one of 'em."

"Wouldn't take much to knock me," I said.

"Sure as hell wouldn't," he said, grinning. "Get your ass outa here. I can't think good with you around."

I didn't argue. I decided I'd go see if I could get Lonzo's Hudson started; he didn't care for me using it if I could. He must not have tried it himself, because it started right off for me. On the way to Thalia I met Granddad, driving along the highway as slow as the big Lincoln would go. He knew he was getting pretty old to be driving, and he took it pretty easy. When I got back to the ranch myself, eight hours later, I had seen the first night of the rodeo. It was a slow, dragging show, but I had a lot of fun fooling around behind the chutes, talking to Hermy and the other boys. I even found a girl to take to the dance, and we stayed till it was over. When I got home I was pretty well worn out. The house was dark, and my sheets were hot. I went to the bathroom and got a glass of water and sprinkled them down, but the night was sultry hot, and they didn't stay cool.

3.

I was sitting up in bed. A wild yell woke me. At first I was groggy, and I thought I had dreamed it, but then I heard it again and I knew it was Hud. It was bright moonlight outside, but I couldn't tell where the yelling was coming from. I got out of bed and felt around for my clothes. I thought he had been staggering around drunk and got on a rattlesnake. As soon as I found my boots I hurried down to the kitchen and put them on. Then I got the big flashlight out of the pantry, and the twenty-two out of the gun closet. But it was so light in the back yard I really didn't need the flashlight, and I shoved it in my hip pocket. The dogs were standing by the yard gate, listening and growling. Then I heard Hud's voice again, loud and rough in the still night. He wasn't yelling any more, he was just talking loud. He was in Halmea's room. The light was on. I heard his voice again, and I started for the room. I saw the yellow patch of light that fell on her wooden steps. My legs were trembly, and I put a shell in the chamber. I knew what I'd see when I got there, but I didn't know what I could do. When I was halfway down the trail I saw Jesse step quickly into the light and go inside; he just had on his pants and undershirt. Then I heard Halmea crying and trying to say something, but her voice got mixed with Hud's, and the sound they made was very loud against the stillness of the pastures.

I didn't go to the door, like Jesse had. I went to the window. I could see them as plain as day, not two yards from me, Hud and Halmea. They were on the bed, and Hud had wrestled her part way under him. Halmea's face was turned toward me, she was trying to curl toward the wall; her eyes were shut, and the squeezed-out tears wet her cheeks. She was trying to jab at Hud with her elbow, to roll away from him, but he wouldn't let her. He had made her naked from her feet to her breasts, and he was laying across her brown twisting legs, trying to catch her hand. He had his cheek against her side, but he raised up, and I saw that he was grinning his old wild grin. He kept shoving at Halmea's white nightgown, trying to shove it over her head, but it was all wadded up around her breasts. I couldn't see Jesse anywhere, and I raised the twenty-two and pointed it at Hud. Then Hud laughed, his teeth white and strong in his whiskered face. "Now, you bitch," he said, and I knew I ought to shoot him and I knew I couldn't. Halmea's eyes were still shut and her mouth was twisted, but she didn't try to holler. "Just rest easy," Hud said. He smothered her arm against his chest and brought his hand over her shoulder and hit her with the heel of it, hard in the face, like he might hit a mare and she grunted with the hurt of it, and gritted her teeth as if she thought he was about to hit her again. Blood came in the corner of her mouth, but she was still trying to roll and kick. "Wild bitch, ain't you?" Hud said, grinning again. He turned her, then, and jammed his big knee down between her naked legs, and he laughed. The blood was pounding through my head so I could barely think. I wanted to shoot Hud and not be afraid of him any longer, but I couldn't think to, I just stood there watching. Then Hud slipped his hand up under the wadded white gown and caught and squeezed one of Halmea's breasts, and then he mashed it and she groaned when he did. She said, "Oooah," and I shot the gun. I shot and the bullet tore through the screen above them and thunked into the wall on the other side of the room. I couldn't shoot to hit him; I guess I thought just any shot would end it. He rolled off Halmea and I saw her brown body twist as she turned toward the wall. Then I cocked the gun and went around to the door, but even before I got there Hud was out and grabbed me, yanked at the screen and shoved me inside, into the yellow light. He was still grinning. "You little fucker," he said. "Come in where you can watch the show." I stumbled on the linoleum, and he was behind me, he shoved or backhanded me, I was on the floor, up against the wall, half under the card table, my eyes still open, the gun on the floor at the foot of the bed. Jesse was laying on the linoleum, by the bed, not moving. Hud shook the tangled hair out of his eyes, his hands at his Levi buttons; he was looking at Halmea—he didn't even glance at Jesse or me. Halmea was curled right against the wall; there was a long raw scratch on her naked back. "Turn over here, nig," Hud said, grinning; he grabbed one of her ankles. "Here's half the menfolks on this ranch come to help you," he said. "The other half's slower and lazier. I guess they'll be along in a minute. I'll stack 'em up two deep 'fore I'm done with you." I sat against the wall, a ringing like a seashell in my head. I wondered where Granddad was, if he was up. Halmea uncurled and began to kick at Hud with both feet; her eyes were open and her bloody lips squeezed tight together. But Hud leaned over and slapped her on the gut with his open hand and the air whoosed out of her mouth and he grabbed her other ankle and pulled her around him while she tried to get wind. Halmea turned her head toward me, and when she did Hud put both hands on her face and held her down while he shoved and shoved, and I could hear her choking for wind and I could hear Hud's breath, but not my own and not Jesse's, and I could see the dark blood from Halmea's mouth trickling down the sheet toward the part of her that was under Hud. I didn't move or blink, but then Hud was standing up grinning at me; he was buckling his ruby belt buckle. "Ain't she a sweet patootie?" he said. He whistled and began to tuck his pants legs into the tops of his red suède boot. Halmea had curled toward the wall, and the blood on the sheets was smeared.

"Now let that be a lesson to you," Hud said. He was calm and loose-looking. He was talking to Halmea, but he held out one hand to me, as if he wanted to help me up. "You keep gallivantin'

aroun' without tellin' me, I'll sure as hell do it agin.
Cause now on, I'm the boss. Not Homer Bannon,
not fantan there, not Ma. Me. Mister Scott. The
boss." He turned and went out the door without
looking back. Before I could move, Halmea jumped
off the bed, her face wilder than Hud's had been.

"Where dat gun?" she said. She grabbed it off the
floor and went to the steps and shot three times into
the darkness. She quit, and I heard Hud laughing.
She shot twice more and clicked the gun two or
three times before she knew it was empty; then she
dropped it on the steps and went back to the bed.
We heard the rough roar of Hud's mufflers, the last
time I ever heard them.

Halmea was wiping the blood off her mouth with
the sheet, and I began to get up. She squatted down
and bent over Jesse, rolled him on his back. When
she did he put out a hand like he wanted to be
helped up, but his eyes were still shut. I saw a big
reddening spot on his jaw. Halmea sat down and
propped his head on her leg.

"Honey, if you okay, wet me a rag," she said, not
looking up. I found one hanging over the lavatory,
and dampened it for her. When she rubbed Jesse's
face he began to blink a little, but he wasn't
conscious.

"He got hit bad," she said. "Just as he come in de
do'."

I wet the rag again, and finally we got Jesse to
open his eyes. He didn't say a word; he sat against

the edge of the bed and put one hand up to shade himself from the yellow light. Halmea went to the lavatory to wash the blood out of her mouth. When she came back we helped Jesse stand up.

"Can't clear my head," he whispered. I let him lean on me. "I need to lie down awhile, I think I'd be all right," he said. Halmea took one arm and I took another and we managed to ease him down the steps. He seemed a little steadier then, and she went back. He held onto me and I helped him across the dark chicken yard to the bunkhouse. "I'm gonna lose my beer," he said. "Can't get my head back on right." When I got him to his cot he began to pull off his undershirt. "Much oblige," he said. "Oh me." He lay back and I turned off the lights and went out into the cool. My own head was throbbing and my neck was stiff, but I felt clear.

Halmea hadn't turned the light out in her cabin, so I went back to see what I could do. She was laying on the bed where Hud had just had her, her face in the crook of one arm. She snuffled something when I spoke at the door, and I went in. She didn't look around, and I didn't know anything to say. I sat down on the edge of the bed and waited. I could see the wetness glisten on her wrists and hands. In a minute she felt me on the bed and looked up, her eyes red and puffed.

"Ise sho down," she said.

"It's over," I said, patting her lightly on the shoulder. I saw three or four cut places on her shoulder and side, where Hud had scratched her in the scuffle. Blood was sticking to her cotton nightgown.

"Oh, it oveh," she said. "Lot a good dat do."

"He was just so drunk," I said.

"Shit," she said, and she sat up suddenly, her lip turned down so I could see the gash on its underside. "Don't gimme dat drunk talk. Mistah Hud wasn't drunk. An' drunk don't mean he can come in an' do dat to somebody."

Her face was beginning to puff where he had hit her, and it occurred to me that she might be hurt really bad. I went and got the washrag for her—it was all the medicine in the cabin—but she was too mad and stirred up to use it.

"Should I take you to town?" I said. "Do you need a doctor?"

"Hush," she said. She stood up, looking so beaten and raw and tired that I didn't know what to do. "I'm gonna wash dem cuts," she said, not noticing the clean rag I had just wet for her. She got another one, but she couldn't reach the cut on her back. I took the rag from her and daubed it clean, while she held her nightgown up.

"I bettah get my suitcase," she said. "I leavin' in de mornin'."

"But you don't need to go," I said. "The law can take care of Hud."

She frowned at me, still raw and angry. "Hush about de law," she said. "No law gonna hear about dis, you see dey don't. Tell de law, dey have it my fault befo' you turn aroun'. I seen dat kinda law befo'."

"But don't run off," I said. "He'll leave you alone."

She snorted. "You see him leave me alone," she said. "He leave me alone good aftah he done wit' me." Then she softened up and began to cry. "Heah, I helpless," she said. "Dat gets me. He come in heah aftah me an' do what he did. Nobody stop him dis time, nobody gonna stop him next time. I seen him come in de do'. Dere I is, I knowed it too. He done told me he'd be dere, plenty times. I thought, dat's just Mistah Hud, he ain't gonna come. But he do come, an' dere you is. Next time he come to dis girl, he gonna have a long trail to follow, I know dat."

"Halmea," I said. "Halmea, don't you go off and leave us. We need you around here. I sure do. I want you to stay."

But she looked farther from me than she ever had. "You get along okay," she said, and it wasn't me, her old honey, she was saying it to. "You see," she said. So I left her and picked up the gun and the flashlight and took them back where they belonged.

I went up to my room and undressed and got in bed, but I didn't even think about going to sleep. My head had started aching, and I felt a little sick at my stomach. I kept seeing Halmea stretched on her bed naked, and Hud wrestling her under him. I knew he didn't do it because he was drunk. He did it because he wanted to get her down and job it in her. I knew he wanted to get Halmea; he'd told me so plenty of times. I remembered how she was crying that night he got home from Temple; how he had caught her in the kitchen and pinched her teats. What bothered me was I had wanted to do pretty much the same thing to Halmea. I didn't want to do it mean, like Hud did everything, but I wanted to do it to her. I was shaking, lying there in bed. And Hud would always do the thing he wanted to do, whether it hurt anybody or not; Hud just did what he intended to do. Watching him screw Halmea, I should have killed him, but I didn't. I stood back and I waited. Wanted to watch. I was shaking more, lying there. I did like Halmea so much; she was one of the best people there ever was, and I could see her so many different ways when she was the Halmea I liked. But now I could only see her naked, pinned there on the bed, like a heifer Hud had thrown down to work over or to splay; I could see her haunch and her breasts and Hud grabbing at her ankles. It made me feel sorry for her and yet want to watch at the same time; and I got more miserable, turning over and over trying to get comfortable. Finally I shoved open the screen and vomited down the side of the house. I was thinking how I wanted to do good things for Halmea and never do a mean thing to her, but I couldn't get over wanting to wallow her. I thought of her that day she brought the lemonade and set it by my bed when I felt sick; and I remembered the streak of flour had been white on her forehead. I wanted to thank her for that and do something nice for her on account of it. But even thinking about the lemonade, what I remembered most, more than the tall sweaty glass or the icy juice or her cool fingers on my forehead, was the dark tight tops of her breasts as she stooped over. Thinking of all that made me want to cry, and I turned over again and wished I could find a way to get peace. I wished I could get together with Halmea somewhere way off from the ranch, where we could just talk. If we could, I might think of a way to let her know all the different things I thought about her that night; maybe she would have known what was silly about them, and what was right and good. Anyway, we could have talked. Finally, my head eased a little, and I quit tossing and turning and worrying so much. The moon was still high up in the west, shedding its faint white light over Granddad's pastures, and I lay with my face to the window watching the night till I fell to sleep.

4.

Halmea cooked breakfast in her town clothes the next morning. We were a tired-looking bunch, all of us except Grandma; she was as full of energy as ever. Hud wasn't there, and Jesse was feeling too bad to eat much. Granddad took it all in, but he didn't ask any questions while we were eating. We were drinking our coffee when Halmea came in and gave notice.

"I needs to be leavin' today," she said. "If Mistah Lonnie or somebody kin haul me inta town. I can stay till somebody else comes if you-all just have to have me, but I needs to leave today."

"Why goodness," Granddad said. "Why you quittin' us so sudden? Ain't we been treatin' you right?"

"Some is," she said, not looking at him. "But I needs to go."

"Now I wouldn't do that," Jesse said. "I think things will be all right. No use you worryin'."

"I ain't worryin'," she said. "Ise just quittin'."

She washed the dishes and I drove her into Thalia. Grandma took on about it some, but Halmea didn't pay her any mind at all. During the ride in, we both kept pretty quiet. She seemed awful far away, still blank and raw outside and in.

"What you gonna do?" I said finally. "Just sit home?"

"I get me a job someplace," she said. "I'm gonna take a trip, de first thing. I spect I go see my sistah in Oklahoma City. Might just stay up dere an' work."

Every day the Trailways Bus stopped in Thalia, and it had Oklahoma City on the sign in front of it. But to me it was just another of those unseen towns down the highway, a place where some roads ended and others began. I couldn't imagine Halmea living there.

I pulled up in front of the little unpainted house where her aunt lived, and helped her carry the few bags and boxes up to the porch. Her aunt was in the side yard, hoeing her garden; she was chopping the tomato plants along with the goat-heads and weeds. She was so blind and deaf she didn't even notice us all the time we were moving the boxes.

"Ain't she a sight," Halmea said. "She choppin' dem pea vines like dey wus weeds." She stood on the steps, and I stood below her in the brown, clean-swept yard, my hands empty. She kept fiddling with the belt on her blue-and-white dress.

"You tell you grandpa I sholy sorry to leave," she said. "Specially to leave so quick like. But I just needs to go. Help him out, he gettin' old an' feeble now. He your job all de time." She seemed so blue and sad, and I knew she wished I'd go on home; but I was choked up and I hated to leave. "You get into town, why, come an' see me," she said. "You be welcome."

"When you leavin'?" I asked.

"Leavin' where?" she said.

"To go to Oklahoma City."

"Oh lawdy," she said, "I just said dat. I may not go anywhere. An' den I may. I be here awhile." She grinned a puffy grin at me and stepped up on the old board porch. "Go on to work," she said. "Don't be lazy."

"Well, I'll see you," I said. "You take it easy."

She nodded, and I got in and drove on to town, to the pool hall. I intended to put in the morning shooting, but the place was empty except for Dumb

Billy. I didn't feel like practicing, so I went on home.

I didn't figure Granddad would have anything to do, but my figuring was off. It turned out to be a good thing for me that the pool hall was empty. When I got to the ranch my horse was saddled and tied to the feed rack, and there was a note fluttering from the note pin on the lot gate. It didn't take long to read:

> Lonnie—
> Come on to the West pasture. We got to round the cattle up again. Get you a big drink, it will be a miserable day.
>
> Your Granddad

When I was mounted, I noticed the bulldozers. There were eight or ten of them, sitting out in the old grown-over field we never used. By the time I was a mile from the barn they had cranked up, and you could hear them all over the prairie. Huge clouds of dust began to roll out of the fields, and I knew they must be scraping out pits. Even so, I didn't believe it. I didn't believe Granddad had given up, and I still didn't believe it when I saw him.

But whether he had or not, he was right about the day. We rounded them all up again, and worked till after dark to do it. Only this time, when we came in worn out and hungry, there wasn't any Halmea to serve us steak and beans and cherry pie.

CHAPTER

10

The room was still dark when I felt Granddad's hand on my shoulder. "Time to get up, son," he said. I turned over, but I didn't think I could possibly get up and work without a little more sleep. There wasn't the least sign of morning in the yard; the moon hung somewhere over the house, still covering the pastures with dim milky light.

I was asleep, but I got up anyway and staggered around dressing. When I got downstairs, Granddad was standing by the stove, frying eggs, and the men were just coming in the back door. Hank Hutch was with them, and he began to help Granddad with the cooking. The bawling that had gone on all night was sparser now, the old cows finally bedded down. I drank some milk and began to put away bacon and eggs. Granddad finally left the stove and ate, without saying a word. Hud was not there.

Granddad was the first one through with breakfast, and the rest of us had to hurry our coffee and follow him out of the house. Dawn was still aways off, but a timid grayness was coming in the eastern sky. We caught our horses in the dark lots, and led them out to be saddled. Then I saw several sets of headlights coming across the pastures; the drivers were honking, trying to get the old cows to move out of the road.

"Here they come," Granddad said. "At least they'll be on time." He sighed heavily, fiddling with his flank girt. "I'd rather take a beatin'," he said.

There was nothing to do but mount up and start the cattle toward the pits. It was just light enough then that I could see the brush, and make out the cattle, where they stood in bunches in the early mist. I went on the very outside of the pasture, right next to the fence, and shoved the cattle down to the inside men. The horse pasture was only a section, and it didn't take very long to go around it. The line of men inside shouted and yelled, to keep the cattle moving, and the cows moved off in strings toward the big tank. Behind me the rim of the plain was reddening, the sun creeping close to the surface. I topped a little ridge, the highest ground in the pasture, and saw the whole drive spread out below me. The first red streamers of light were dusty and brilliant on the green mesquite. Banks of mist rose from the dewy grass and hung gray around the bellies of the moving cattle. Hank was next to me; Jesse next to him; then Lonzo, popping the reins of his bridle against his chaps; Cecil Goad and his

171

boys farther away; and Granddad, small and far-
thest of all, sitting on the other side of the tank
watching his herd come down to water. I could hear
Cecil yelling at the cattle: "Commence agoing."
When we got to the tank the cows and calves
walked into the shallows, splashing the clean gold
sheet of the tank. They were already slinging slobber over their shoulders at the flies. Less than a mile
away the pits were waiting. It was like a picture: me,
the men, the fresh leafy range, the Bannon herd
trailing into water, Granddad watching. I rode on
to the tank and let my horse splash in among the
cows. Granddad sat above me on the dam, his
hands folded on the saddle horn, his horse standing
quiet. The sun flashed on Stranger's bright coat,
and showed Granddad burning clear. Then he
waved at Hank and Jesse, and I whirled to the
drive. Horses and cattle stirred the water to foam.
We left the tank, and in no time were almost to the
pits. Granddad dropped out of the drive when we
went past the barn. I figured he went after the two
longhorns and the old bull. He had shut them up
the night before. But he came back with just the
two milk cows. With all the help we had the cattle
were easy to handle. Then the pits were in front of
us, gaping in the old rocky field, each pit with one
end sloped and one end steep. The cattle paid them
little mind; they went right on down the sloped
ends, curious to see what they'd find at the bottom.

I was stationed at the slope end of the next to last

pit west. I was supposed to keep anything from
coming back up. Cecil Goad's boy held the pit next
to mine. The cattle were standing quietly in the
bottom, the calves sucking, the cows licking themselves and their calves. Then one of the state men
came up behind me and stepped to the edge of the
pit. He had a clip-action rifle in his hand; a
thirty-ought-six.

"Hi, son," he said. "I hope this won't shy your
horse."

"It may," I said. "I never shot off him atall."

He was a short, gray-headed man, as nice as his
job would let him be. "Ride off a little piece when I
start shootin'," he said. "Won't nothin' come outa
this pit." He spread a rag on the ground and laid
several extra clips on it, glancing ever minute or so
at the cattle. "Fine bunch a cows," he said.

Then the first shot sounded behind us, and my
horse jumped and reared. The man dropped on one
knee and began shooting, and the hungry young
heifers fell. In a second I couldn't hear anything for
the sound and the bawling; all I could do was fight
my snorting horse as close to the pit mouth as
possible. The guns went off constantly, and the
horse was crazy with scare. Finally he hung his
head and stood quivering, every muscle tight. Dust
rose from the pits so thick it was a miracle the
gunners could see to shoot. The cattle below bunched tight together, bellering and milling in a
welter of dust and blood. Nothing did them any

good. The man with the gun was deadly. The second one clip emptied he had another one in and was leveling the gun. The biggest old cows fell like they had been sledge-hammered; they kicked a time or two, belched blood into the dust, lay still. Not one in my pit got up. A calf dashed toward us and the man swung the gun and knocked it back on the body of a horned cow, its hind legs jerking. The old cows rolled their ·eyes and spun around and around. Not for a minute did the dust or noise settle. Finally the last animal in the pit stood facing us, a big heifer. She was half hemmed in by the sprawled carcasses. She took one step toward us, head up, and the man fired, slamming her backward like a telephone pole had bashed her between the eyes. She lay on her side, one foreleg high in the air. The man took out his clip and went quickly to another pit, to help. I was as tight as my horse; I was sick of the heat, and of the dust smells and gunpowder and thin manure. I tried to spit the putrid taste out of my mouth, and couldn't. The flies were already buzzing around the hot carcasses, the shit bugs swarming on the green puddles. The Goad boy was vomiting all over a young mesquite bush, but I didn't feel sick that way; I just felt suffocated by the dust and sound, like my throat was filling up with sand. I saw Granddad, sitting on Stranger at the head pit. He pointed and some gunner sent another bullet into some straining animal. The noise began to scatter, just a finishing shot or two. Granddad was sitting still, his hands on the saddle horn. For a second all I could hear was the scraping bolts, as the gunners cleared their magazines. Then it was silent and hot.

Jesse was on his horse, at the third pit; he was talking to Hank Hutch. I rode by him on my way to the barn, and heard him talking in a watery voice, but what he said got away from me. Hank loped up beside me before I got to the barn, and we rode in together.

"Didn't take long," I said.

He was the quietest I'd ever seen him. "Don't take very long to kill things," he said. "Not like it takes to grow."

The rest of the men rode up behind us. They tied their horses and we all walked over to the water trough to drink. The two old steers and the old bull stood in the little feed pen, lazily pulling oat straw out of the hayrack. Mr. Burris and his driver walked up while we were drinking the cold water, and I offered him a cup. He drank and handed the cup to Thompson. In a minute Granddad tied Stranger and came over.

"Well, I was agonna keep them three," he said, pointing to the old cattle. "But I guess it wouldn't do much good; they'd just get lonesome. Three head ain't much of a herd."

"And they ain't none a them cows," he added, pulling off his gloves.

"They make good animals to have around,"

Hank said. "They remind you of the time when the government didn't have to run a man's business for him."

Granddad shook his head. "Hell," he said. "If the time's come when I got to spend my time lookin' back, why, I'd just as soon go under. I ain't never got much kick outa my recollections. Maybe I'll learn, I don't know."

"Goddamn," Thompson said. "We missed three. You-all stay here, I'll take care of 'em." He started toward his car.

"Where do you think you're agoin', Mister," Granddad said. Thompson stopped and looked at him, unsure.

"To finish this job," he said. "Somebody needs to."

"You just come back here," Granddad said. "I'll kill them three myself, seein' as I raised 'em. Get me the rifle, son," he said to me.

But Thompson fidgeted. He didn't quite have the nerve to go on after his gun, but he wanted to awful bad. "There ain't no guarantee you'd do it," he said.

"I just said I would," Granddad said.

"Shit," Thompson said, turning toward his car.

He had his hand on the door when Mr. Burris came awake. "You get in that car," he said. "We're going down and see about burning these carcasses, and then we're leaving. Mr. Bannon can take care of the rest of this without us bothering him."

I stepped to the pickup and got the thirty-thirty

we kept behind the seat, to use on coyotes. There were shells in it, but I got a box out of the glove compartment, just in case. Thompson got in the Chevy and said no more, but Mr. Burris still stood by the water trough, looking uncomfortable. He was twisting one of the leather buttons on his jacket. We could all feel him straining for something to say.

"Now you go on, Mr. Burris," Granddad said quietly. "I know this here ain't your doin's. I imagine you got enough worries without takin' on any a mine. I'll last over this here. You just see about the burnin', and then get that feller there off my ranch."

"Well, all I can say is I'm sorry," Mr. Burris said. "I'm sure sorry."

"So'm I," Granddad said. "Things are just put together wrong. There's so much shit in the world a man's gonna get in it sooner or later, whether he's careful or not. But you go ahead, we ain't mad at you." He held out his hand, and he and Mr. Burris shook.

"Well, I'll be back to see you about the payments," Mr. Burris said. He got in and they drove off, dust hanging over the car.

"He ain't such a bad feller," Granddad said. "Just got a shitter of a job." He came over and took the gun from me. Then he went to the feed pen, Jesse and Hank and me following. The two old outlaws stood across the lot from us, as far away as they could get, the bright morning sun flashing on their horns. The old cherry-backed bull still stood by the hayrack, his eyes shut, chewing the yellow oat straw slowly. Tiny sprigs of hay clung to his white dewlap.

"They'll never grow stock like them old fieries agin," Hank said. Granddad stood with one hand in his pocket, the other holding the gun.

"I never will," he said. "Lord, but I've chased them two steers many a mile." His voice was even. "I don't know if I can kill 'em," he said. "But I guess I can. Goddamnit. I'll just do it right here and you fellers can tie onto 'em an' drag 'em down about the hill somewhere to burn 'em. You-all go to the pump and draw me three five-gallon cans a gas, so we can burn 'em quick. I'll handle this end of the operation."

The other men were sitting around the corner of the barn, not saying much. We didn't speak to them as we went by.

"I don't think he'll kill those cattle," I said to Jesse. "He's had 'em too long." We found some cans in the smokehouse and went to the pump, all of us listening for the shots.

"Yes, he will," Hank said. "He'll do it for sure."

Then, with two cans full and the third filling, we heard the first sharp shot, and its echo bouncing back off Idiot Ridge. All the bloody smells of the morning came back on me, and I got the weak trembles. I imagined the old steer in the lots, knocked to his side, the old horns closer and closer

178

to the dust. And Granddad, as old as the steer, sighting down the bright barrel. I sat down by one of the gas cans, on the short dusty grass.

"I told you he would," Hank said.

Jesse watched the gas pump and didn't say anything. Then the second shot came, and there was only one to wait for.

"Just the bull left," Hank said. "Piss on it, we might as well go back."

Old Domino left then, still standing at the hay-rack eating the yellow hay. Then I saw that Jesse and Hank were gone, and I got up to follow. Hank had taken my can.

We got to the water trough and two shots came; came fast as the gun could lever, and their echoes bouncing off the ridge as one. The four of them were in the lot, Granddad squatting by the fallen bull, his hands clasped between his knees, his old felt hat pulled down. The rifle leaned against the hayrack.

"Took two shots," Hank said. "Them old bulls is hard to kill."

I trailed one hand in the water, wetting my shirt sleeve. I thought he might as well be dead with them, herd and herdsman together, in the dust with his cattle and Grandmother and his old foreman Jericho Green. Then Granddad came out of the lots, the gun in his hand. The steers and the bull lay where we all could see them, the flies free at last to crawl on their unmoving heads. All of us stood by the fence: Jesse and Hank, Lonzo, Cecil and Clement, Silas and John. "Burn the sonsabitches," Granddad said. He handed me the thirty-thirty, and turned to the neighbors. "Much obliged, you fellers," he said. "Until you're better paid." Then he walked to the house.

CHAPTER

11

I went into town that night, hoping the second rodeo performance would be better than the first. I asked Granddad if he wanted to go with me, but he just shook his head. He hadn't said two words to anybody since the killing. Right after supper both he and Granny went to bed. The killing seemed to take as much starch out of Granny as it did out of the rest of us—or maybe what did it with her was having to cook for a change. She drove into Thalia to hire somebody, but she hadn't found a girl that suited her.

When I got to the rodeo arena a long line of people were filing by the ticket office. As I walked through the hundreds of parked cars I saw the cowboys beginning their night. They stood in groups by the open turtlebacks, drinking cans of cold beer. The girls stood with them, shaking their combed heads and peeping at themselves in the rear-view mirrors. The contestants who were really in rodeo for the money were squatting on the ground checking their rigging; but most of the boys were just there for beer and excitement. I saw Irene talking to a bunch of girls, and thought maybe I'd hunt her up later on in the night. I wanted to get the ranch completely off my mind.

I already had my ticket, so I walked in and headed for the bucking chutes. I knew most of the boys would be there, sizing up the bulls and talking. Riding a bull was the kind of thing you did to prove you didn't give a shit. Going past the Sno-Cone stand I ran into Hermy. We stood there a minute watching a couple of drunk cowboys try to date the pretty black-haired woman who was making the hot dogs. Hermy hit me on the shoulder.

"When you-all movin' out?" he said.

I was watching the cowboys, and I didn't understand him. "Hell, I just came in," I said.

"Naw," he said. "I mean Hud's deal."

"You got me," I said. "I don't know what you're talkin' about."

"No shit?" he said. He began to fiddle with his belt buckle and kick his boot toe in the dirt. "Maybe I shouldn't be spreadin' rumors," he said.

"What'd he do?" I said. "Is he in jail?"

"Not by a long shot. He's around on the north side of the arena, sittin' in a new Cadillac. And he ain't the only one sittin' in it."

"Who else?" I said.

"The prettiest bitch you ever saw," he said. "Truman Peters' wife."

I just shook my head. I didn't doubt it for a minute. "Yeah," Hermy said. "This'll knock you on your ass. They say he screwed Truman some way and sold him part of your Granddad's ranch. Won a lot of money off Truman in a card game and went and bought the car and came back and got Truman a little drunker and sold him some kind of crazy option on the ranch."

"Aw, I don't believe that," I said. "He couldn't a sold anything. Even Truman Peters wouldn't fall for anything like that." Truman was an oilman, a multimillionaire, reckless as hell with his money. His wife had been a movie star before she married Truman.

"A lot of 'em say it wasn't legal," Hermy said. "But some of 'em say Hud's just slick enough to get away with it."

"Naw, it couldn't a been legal," I said. But knowing Hud, I didn't feel too sure. When he was running wide open he was a hard man to stop, and with Granddad so discouraged over the herd, and old anyway, I didn't know if he could set Hud down again.

"Anyhow," Hermy said, "Hud's supposed to a won $80,000 dollars from Truman just playin' cards."

"I'm going around an' see him," I said. "Come go with me."

"No," he said. "I got a bull to ride in the first

go-round. Better be careful. They say Truman's gonna be after Hud with a gun for runnin' off with his wife."

"You be careful," I said. "You're the one's gonna be on a bull."

It didn't take me long to find the Cadillac. It was a long cream-colored job, parked right next to the bandstand where the little high-school band was warming up. Hud and the woman weren't even facing the arena.

"Hey," I said. "Can I talk to you a minute?"

He turned from her and squinted at me. "Why hello, hotrod," he said. "What's with you?"

"I won't bother you long," I said.

"You goddamn sure won't," he said. "Come around here and get in."

I got in the front seat, beside them. The car was dark and cool on the inside, smelling of new leather upholstery and whiskey. Hud was smooching the woman, but he broke off when I got in.

"You remember his dad, don't you, Lily?" he said. "Dan Bannon. The pride a the fuckin' prairie." She and I looked at each other through the dimness. She was an awful pretty woman, I thought. Her long blond hair fell down past her shoulders, and she looked at me without smiling. Hud had unbuttoned the front of her red dress, and I could see the tops of her breasts and the white cups of her brassière, the rodeo lights from above us throwing a strange glow across her on her hair. She had grown up in a little town near Thalia.

"Aw yea," she said. "I remember Dan. Me and him was sweethearts about two weeks one time." She laid her hand on Hud's leg. Hearing her mention my father made the hair bristle on my neck.

"If you're pissed off, get your ass out," Hud said. "No, I ain't really sold the ranch, but I got some money for it. When I do get it from Homer, then I'll see whether Truman can have it or not. The nice thing is, don't nobody but me know what I've done." The woman's dress was wadded up in her lap, and Hud was rubbing her long bare leg, his hand sliding up and down.

"You moving us off?" I asked, and he leaned back and laughed.

"You ain't that lucky," he said. "Hell, no. If I do ever sell Truman the land I got a deal rigged where I can lease it back. It's the funniest goddamn thing you ever heard. By the time they get this deal unraveled I may be as old an' worn out as Homer Bannon. Nobody knows whether the place is mine or Truman's or Homer's."

"Hon, you could sell Truman heaven if you got him drunk enough," the woman said. She turned toward Hud, and the strange gold glow from the lights fell on the soft tops of her breasts. She put her mouth against Hud's shirt and giggled. "You better watch little Dan," she said. "He thinks you're mean."

Hud squeezed her against him and winked at me over her head. "Hell, I am mean," he said. "Didn't you know that?" She looked up and kissed him, and I got out and walked away.

I thought I ought to at least go out and tell Granddad what was going on. Hud was acting so crazy it wouldn't hurt Granddad to be on his guard. When I went back behind the chutes I saw Hermy, still peeping through the board fence at the bulls. He looked nervous.

"I kinda wish I'd stayed outa this bull ridin'," he said.

"You'll never learn any younger," I said. I thought a little hurrahing might cheer him up. "Maybe you won't have to ride very far."

"Eat shit," he said. "I don't feel too good."

I thought Jesse might want to go to the ranch with me, and I asked a couple of cowboys if they'd seen him. He wasn't any trouble at all to find, because he was at the concession stand, eating an orange Sno-Cone and talking to the pretty blackheaded woman. It didn't take field glasses to see that he wasn't getting any encouragement to go on talking.

When he saw me he reached out and put his arm around me; he was drunk enough to be a little extra friendly.

"Did you hear about Hud's deal?" I said. We walked over to the arena and leaned on the fence.

"I heard about ten versions of it," he said. "Looks like somebody showed their ass, but I don't know who." The way he was acting made me a little mad. He had entered the colt in the cutting horse contest to give him some experience, and now he was getting too drunk to ride.

"Look at that boy get busted," he said, watching the show. I couldn't even see the show; I kept seeing the woman's white breasts, and Hud's hand on the heavy part of her leg.

"I'm going out to tell Granddad," I said. "You do what you want to."

"No, I wouldn't go worry that old man," he said. "Don't add no more load on him right now. I don't believe Scott actually sold anything anyway."

"I better go tell Granddad," I said, but Jesse just wasn't paying me any attention.

"I need a can a beer," he said.

"Are you goin' get drunk before you ride?" I said, and he laughed. It was a painful kind of laugh, like something has stung him, or torn inside him.

"I can ride when I'm drunkest," he said. "Some a these nights I'll have to tell you about a ride or two I made."

He wasn't talking to me, really, and I walked off from him. I felt like I was smothering in the crowd. The lights and the giggling and the kids with Sno-Cone on their chins and the drunk cowboys— all of it made me feel like I was strangling. Jesse hanging on the fence half-drunk depressed me, and Hermy about to risk his ass on a bull he knew he couldn't ride depressed me more. It looked like Hud was the only one doing any good for himself. I got in the pickup and drove out of town, and when I was moving down the dark highway, moving on like the song said, I didn't feel so hemmed up and I kinda relaxed. Driving could do that for me a lot of times.

The ranch house was dark, and I knew it had been dark ever since I left. Granddad would be sound asleep, and it would be a hard job waking him up and getting him to understand the news I brought. Standing a minute in the kitchen, I missed Halmea. I wished I had her to tell it all to, so I wouldn't have to wake up Granddad. But I was there, and I went down the hall and into Granddad's room before my nerve failed me. Moonlight from an open window fell in a white puddle on his floor. It lay across the old chifforobe, and touched the silver-edged picture of Grandmother that had stood there since I knew the room. Granddad lay in darkness on the bed. I could hear the heavy whistle of his old man's breath. He was laying on his back, one hand upon his chest.

I came close to him. "Granddad," I said. "Granddad, wake up." I shook his arm gently, and he raised up on one elbow, his eyes open. "That you, Annie?" he said, and for the second time that night my neck hair stood up. He had asked the question to Grandmother. "What is it?" he said, rubbing his eyes with one hand.

"No, me," I said. "Lonnie. I want to talk to you a minute."

"Oh," he said. "Let me get my boots on."

"You don't need to get up," I said. But he got up

anyway, scratching himself through the cotton nightshirt.

"We got to light the lamps," he said, moving slowly to the dresser. "We can't do no talking in the dark." We had electricity, but he had an old kerosene lamp on his dresser that he still used when the power went off. He got it and lit it. The yellow light didn't fill the room; it left high shadows on the walls.

"Sit down, son," he said. "Get you a cheer." He reached in his pocket for his tobacco, but he had on his nightshirt, and it wasn't there. In the yellow lamplight he looked a thousand years old. He was thin-armed, and his eyes set back in shadows. I wished then that I had left him asleep.

"What have you done?" he asked me.

"Not me," I said. "Hud did it. He's trying to sell the ranch."

"Huddie?" he said. He leaned his good ear to me. Just the way he said it made me have to swallow, because I could tell that for some sudden reason he wasn't with me, he was back in another time. I could tell he thought I was my father.

"Hud," I said. "He's tryin' to sell the ranch."

"Is he?" he said. "Oh no, Huddie couldn't sell it. I'm glad you're not in no trouble, Dan. Your ma worries about you some."

"No, Granddad," I said. "Hud is trying to sell it to Truman Peters. Really trying to sell it."

Granddad smiled at me as if it were a joke.

189

"Huddie's a wild one," he said. "His mother's the same way. Ain't nobody ever got no rope on him." He looked at the lamp, and the light made his lined cheeks look yellow. For a minute I think he was with me, in the right night. "He can't sell it," he said. "This here land is mine. I may decide to let him run some of it awhile, I don't know. Right now I just feel like throwing in the sponge and giving up."

That was what I had wanted to hear. "Okay, then," I said. "I'm going on back to the rodeo. You sleep good." I thought maybe he just hadn't been awake at first, but then I knew it wasn't that.

"That's all right," he said. "Just don't worry your ma; she's got enough." He sat on the edge of the bed, smiling at me. Then he took the lamp back to the dresser and blew it out. The moonlight fell back into the room, and Granddad's shadow moved across it. The springs of the old bed creaked. "Just the boy," he said, and the room was quiet.

The talk had been too strange and sad. I thought maybe Granddad had been in a dream, and had stayed in a dream through it all. I saw that the supper dishes were still in the kitchen sink, and for a minute I thought about washing them. But I was feeling like I had in the rodeo crowd, only just the opposite. I wanted to get out of the dark old house with its dreams and ghosts. Granddad was on the other side of a high barbed fence, with each wire a year of life, and I couldn't go over it and I couldn't crawl through. But anyway, I had eased myself a little, and I felt like when I got back to town I could enjoy the rodeo. Only, the worst of all, I wanted Halmea. I wanted to talk to her for a little while. I wasn't as worried about Granddad as I had been; he seemed to be where Hud couldn't hurt him. But driving through the dark alleyways of mesquite, I thought of Halmea, and wished there had been someway to keep Hud from doing what he had. Then I remembered seeing Irene in the car seat, the morning before the rodeo, her hair spread like a scarf. I knew she was at the rodeo, and I decided to try and find her. She wasn't as exciting as Lily, sitting in the Cadillac, but she was who I would look for. After the show was all over, after the dancing and the fiddle music, when the gay riders had all gone off to bed, Irene and I might ride out into the heavy-smelling fields, and stay there awhile. Her black hair would be all the cover we'd need.

CHAPTER

12

1.

The next day was the last of the rodeo, and I didn't much care. The whole crazy circle of things got so it tired me out. When I woke up that morning I could see Jesse down in the lots, moving around, and I got up to go talk to him. I had looked for him the night before, after the dance, but he wasn't around, and I guess he got home on his own.

There was nobody to cook my breakfast, and I didn't feel like cooking it myself. I ate a bowl of cereal and did without anything else. When I got to the barn, Jesse was dragging around cleaning out the horse stalls. A friend of ours who had a little pasture in town was keeping the colt during the rodeo. Jesse looked pretty puny.

"Seen Granddad?" I asked him.

He stopped raking hay and leaned on his hull fork a minute. "He's up an' gone," he said. "He saddled up about an hour ago and rode off west."

"Didn't say where he was going?"

"No, he never," Jesse said. "He said a few other things, though. Said he'd have to let me and Lonzo go. He don't plan on having much work to do for a while."

"Did he mention about Hud?" I said. "I came out an' told him last night."

"Naw, he never," Jesse said. "He said he was sorry he couldn't afford to keep us till times got better. I didn't expect he'd be able to. He ain't allowed to run no cattle for a year."

I remembered how Granddad's mind had strayed into the past the night before. "Did he seem all right this morning?" I asked. "He acted last night like he might be slippin' a little."

"Well, he didn't seem very spry," Jesse said. "But I didn't notice nothin' else."

I left him to his raking and went up to the house. Grandma met me at the door and lit into me to take her to Thalia, so she could look for some help. She had taken herself the day before, whether she could drive or not, but she wasn't in the mood to try it again. I finally had to take her. She went to see a lady who had cooked for us years before, and the lady told her of a girl who might help. We chased the girl down and got her to agree to move out the next day, so Granny was satisfied. I wasn't so happy about it myself. She was a lazy, fattish-looking white girl, and she acted dumber than a turkey.

When we got back, Granddad was sitting by his radio. I asked him where he'd been, and he said he had just wanted to ride around and have a look at his grass—see how much he had. He talked as sensible and reasonable as he ever had, only he was awful blue and depressed.

"I don't know if I got the energy to start it over," he said. "I don't know if I've got the time. Right now I just feel like I've finally wore plumb out. I couldn't hardly drag a saddle this morning. I may just have to sit here till I rot."

"I guess this was the worst thing that ever happened to you, wasn't it?" I said.

He rubbed one hand through his hair, and shook his head. "Oh no," he said. "Not the worst by a long shot. Your grandmother getting killed was a tragedy. Aw, I can get over this here if my health don't go to failing me."

I tried quizzing him about Hud, but he just said he'd have to see him before he'd know anything. He mentioned firing Jesse, but he said he had about changed his mind and decided to keep Lonzo around a little while, if he could. He had decided to build some new fences. Finally Granddad got to where he was paying more attention to the radio than he was to me, and I went upstairs to read. When I came down a little later to eat a bite, I noticed how stiff Granddad got around. It was like his leg joints were sticking on him all of a sudden.

2.

When I left for the rodeo that night, Hud still hadn't come home. There had been no sign of him, or of the Cadillac, and we had no way of knowing whether Truman Peters had caught up with him or not. Jesse and Lonzo went into town together, in Lonzo's old car, so I was left with the pickup.

I was way late getting to the show. On the outskirts of town, like in that song, I saw Buddy Andrews stopped beside the road. He had had some kind of a breakdown, and was out fiddling under his hood. He was as pissed off as he could be. Something had gone wrong with his generator, and he had a hot date for the rodeo. I tied on to him with a chain and pulled him into Thalia, but of course when we got there it turned out all the mechanics had gone to the rodeo, and weren't to be found. Buddy was in the worst mood of his life. We spent about an hour tracking down a colored mechanic, and then another hour getting the car and the mechanic to a garage where he could go to work on it. When I finally left them, Buddy had got his clean clothes greasy, and was trying his best to get the man to hurry. The final performance of the Thalia rodeo was almost over before I even got to the parking area.

I could tell there wasn't much show left, because the musicians were already over on the concrete slab, tuning their fiddles and guitars. The people who didn't like rodeo and just came to dance were filing out of the grandstand and heading for the slab. I went on inside, anyway. The cutting horses were in the arena working, and our colt wasn't with them. I stood by the fence and watched. While I was standing there a kid named Pin came up to me; he was wearing a big black Stetson, and he had a can of beer in one hand. He looked like the rodeo, about nine tenths done.

"Hey, cowboy," he said. "Did you see Hermy?"

"Not tonight," I said. "I just got here. I been helping Andrews fix his car."

"Oh, goddamn, you shoulda been here," he said, belching. "A bull stepped on Hermy. God, he was hollerin' and cussin'."

"No shit?" I said. "Did he get hurt bad?"

Pin nodded and tried to look solemn, but he was enjoying having a story to tell. "The bull stepped right in his stomach," he said. "He wasn't out, though, he was yellin' his fuckin' head off. They say he was broke all to pieces inside. Shit, you ain't gonna see me on one a them bastards." He left, tossing his beer can on the ground with a thousand others. I noticed he had a canvas contestant's sticker pinned to the back of his shirt.

YOUR ATTENTION PLEASE, the announcer said. WILL JESSE LOGAN REPORT TO THE ARENA AT ONCE. LAST CALL FOR JESSE LOGAN. WILL YOU PLEASE BRING YOUR HORSE TO THE CUTTING ARENA AT ONCE. IF NOT, YOU WILL BE

SCRATCHED. YOUR ENTRY WILL BE SCRATCHED. LAST
CALL FOR MR. LOGAN.

I ran around behind the chutes, wondering where
in the world Jesse was. Surely he hadn't gone off
without making the final performance. Then I
found the colt, saddled and ready, tied to the fence.
But no Jesse anywhere. I was almost ready to ride
the colt myself, when I heard the announcer scratch
the horse. I left him tied and walked on around the
arena, figuring Jesse might have got in a fight or got
kicked or something. Somebody yelled at me and I
saw Hud and his new woman coming out of the
grandstand. He was leading her along by the arm.

"Well, now where's your fine feathered friend
tonight?" he said.

"I wish I knew," I said. "Granddad fired him this
morning, he may be gone. The colt's back there
tied."

"Homer fired him? The hell he did." He pulled
Lily to him and snickered something in her ear. She
smiled at what he said. Hud was wild and messed-
up-looking, like he hadn't changed clothes since the
card game, his shirttail out of his pants; but Lily
was wearing a gold and white dress, and her long
honey-and-butter hair curled like a colt's tail down
her back. She looked even prettier than she had in
the Cadillac.

"Well, the sonofabitch just wasted an entry fee,"
Hud said. "Tell him he better not forget he's fired.

197

If I run into him I may take that entry money out in skin."

"Carry me back to the car, honey," the woman said. "I can't wade through this cowshit." Hud picked her up like she was a doll, and she put her face against his neck.

LADIES AND GENTLEMEN, the announcer said, THIS CONCLUDES OUR SHOW FOR TONIGHT. LET ME REMIND YOU ABOUT THE BIG DANCE OVER THERE ON THE SLAB, STARTING RIGHT NOW. FREDDY HILL AND HIS POST OAK VALLEY BOYS WILL BE THERE FURNISHING THE MUSIC, FROM NOW TILL ONE O'CLOCK. ADMISSION IS JUST FIFTY CENTS A HEAD, SO YOU FELLERS GRAB YOUR FILLIES AND GET ON OVER THERE. THANK YOU, LADIES AND GENTLE-MEN, AND WE HOPE TO SEE YOU ALL BACK WITH US NEXT YEAR. OH, EXCUSE ME, he said. WILL YOU KEEP YOUR SEATS JUST A MINUTE? I HAVE SOME NEWS THAT YOU-ALL WILL BE ANXIOUS TO HEAR. THE YOUNG MAN WHO WAS INJURED TONIGHT IN THE BULL-RIDING CONTEST IS NOW BEING TAKEN BY AMBULANCE TO THE HOSPITAL IN WICHI-TA FALLS. THEY WERE UNABLE TO TREAT HIM SATISFAC-TORILY HERE. I KNOW YOU'RE ALL HOPING AND PRAYING THAT THE YOUNG MAN IS ALL RIGHT, AND WE SURE ARE TOO. IF ANY MORE NEWS REACHES US WE'LL GIVE IT TO YOU AT THE DANCE, THANK YOU, AND GOOD NIGHT.

It made me feel weak in the stomach to know that Hermy was bad hurt. Right then, they were racing him across the dark highway in an ambulance. The next morning I would get loose and go visit him, but first I had to find Jesse.

The dance slab was filling up fast. Over the voices and the shuffling, I could hear the band playing "Your Cheating Heart," and the boot soles scraped the concrete in time to it. I passed by a fist fight and stopped a minute to watch. "You're a hot-check-writing bastard," one of the boys said, and they slugged away. I went on. Fist fights would be easy to find. I pushed my way onto the dance floor, and it felt like the whole ranch country was in on it with me. The old men bunched together near the corners, and the little kids, boys and girls both, were out on the dance floor whooping and running. I saw one little boy sound asleep on a bench, with a couple courting right beside him. The rodeo contestants and their girl friends made up a good part of the crowd. Now that the show was over the boys were drunk and excited, hoping the nooky was going to come after the dance, and they really lived it up. The grown-ups two-stepped and single-footed right along to the rock and roll numbers that the band had to play. Now and then there would be a polka or a square dance especially for the old folks. But it wouldn't be long before the old ones would trickle out, and the musicians wouldn't have anyone but the kids to please. Then the dance songs would last longer and go faster. "Hit it there, Leroy," the bandleader said.

I eased my way through the crowd, looking for

Jesse among the sorrowful stag cowboys on the sides. I went around twice without finding him, but I knew he would have been easy enough to miss. Then I ran into a girl I knew, and we danced awhile. She was so looped she barely knew me, but it didn't matter. The cowboy vocalist laid down his fiddle and came to the mike to sing. He sang a new song, one I had only heard a time or two before. It was called "Fräulein."

> Far across the distant waters
> Lived an old German's daughter,
> On the banks of the old River Rhine . . .

I locked my hands and dropped them on the girl's butt, and swayed along with the music and forgot Jesse for a minute. The people were quieting down a little, and the singer was crying into the mike about the girl him and all the other soldier boys had left alone across the waters. "That's too slow," Charlene said, looking up at me. "I want somethin' fast, make a little whoopee, don't you?" But she got quiet again. The mournfulness of the song was getting to me, but before I had really caught it bad they switched to a polka and I led Charlene to the side. While we were watching the old folks jig around, a tired-looking cowboy waltzed up to us with a blonde. "Here, you can have this one," he said, holding out the girl's arm. "I don't want her no more; I'll take yours." I told him he was welcome to all I had, and walked away. They were all too drunk to know what became of me.

Since I wasn't finding anybody in the dance, I went outside and walked through the parking lot awhile. The pickup wasn't very far from the dance floor, and I went to it. There was a wagon sheet in the back. I got in and unrolled part of it and stretched out on my back. I thought maybe Jesse might come by, and waiting would be the quickest way to find him. The band was playing one of those songs of Hank Williams', the one about the wild side of life, and the music floated over the car tops and touched me. I felt lost from everybody, and from myself included, laying on a wagon sheet in a pastureland of cars. Only the tune of the song reached me, but the tune was enough. It fit the night and the country and the way I was feeling, and fit them better than anything I knew. What few stories the dancing people had to tell were already told in the worn-out words of songs like that one, and their kind of living, the few things they knew and lived to a fare-thee-well were in the sad high tune. City people probably wouldn't believe there were folks simple enough to live their lives out on sentiments like those—but they didn't know. Laying there, thinking of all the things the song brought up in me, I got more peaceful. The words I knew of it, about the wild side of life, reminded me of Hud and Lily, but more than that, the whole song reminded me of Hermy and Buddy and the other boys I knew. All of them wanted more and seemed to end up with less; they wanted excitement and ended up stomped by a bull or smashed against a highway; or they wanted a girl to court; and anyway, whatever it was they wanted, that was what they ended up doing without. That song ended, and another one began, and it ended, and then I got up and went back into the dark arena to untie the colt and take him to his pen. I thought maybe I would come back to the dance and honky-tonk a little myself.

3.

Before I got near the horse, I heard Jesse talking. He was sitting spraddle-legged against the fence, talking to the horse. There were three or four empty beer cans scattered around his feet.

"Everbody's gone home but me," he said. "If anybody's left it's always me."

When I squatted down beside him he didn't seem a bit surprised.

"Hello," he said. "I had her, but she got away."

"Who got away?" I said. I had a pretty good idea.

"That pretty little woman," he said. "We were in somebody's car, just talking, and I took a little nap, dozed off a few minutes. I woke up an' she wasn't there." He sighed, and started to get up. "But I been left many a time," he said. "I didn't wake up in time to ride the colt, either. I just fucked up."

"It don't make too much difference," I said.

"Makes a little," he said. I saw that he wasn't

really drunk, he was just trying to be, or wishing he was. "Oh, the colt wouldn't a won," he said. "But it woulda made a little difference to me. Reason I came up here in the first place, I got drunk an' fell off a cuttin' horse. In the San Antone show. Ladybug went one way and Jesse went the other."

"Hell, so what," I said. He was feeling real sorry for himself about something. "Falling off a horse ain't much of a crime," I said.

"No," he said. He was fiddling with the colt's reins. "Fallin' off wasn't no crime. It wasn't even a disgrace. My boss didn't think so either. He give me three hundred dollars and told me to haul Ladybug home. But you know," he said. "I never done it. I got to thinking about it and got drunk agin, and went up the road about sixty miles an' turned the trailer over an' broke that little mare's neck. That was the crime of it. Third best cuttin' horse in the nation, an' she was just a five-year-old. Let's go to the dance," he said. "I want to watch them pretty girls whirl."

I told him I'd meet him there. I got on the colt and took him to the pen and unsaddled him. The dance wasn't but a half a mile away, and I walked back through the cool quiet streets. I could hear the music plain as a radio, and I wasn't all hemmed-up in the crowd. When I got back, Jesse was leaning on the wire fence, looking in.

"Let's stay till the music stops," he said. "This here fascinates me."

The music was slower by that time, with just a

couple of dozen couples pushing themselves around the dance floor. It was after one o'clock, and the bandleader was ready to quit. Some of the cowboys weren't tired, and they wouldn't let the bandleader stop. Jesse stood there nearly thirty minutes, nodding his head to the slow music. I sat on the fender of somebody's car. After they had played "Good Night, Ladies" three times the cowboys gave up and everybody straggled out.

"We might go get a bite to eat," Jesse said. "I ain't goin' back out to you-all's place. Found a trucker, an old boy I used to rodeo with. He said he'd give me a ride to New Mexico early in the mornin' if I'm here. Guess I better sleep in the truck, so I won't miss it."

We went to the pickup, and I drove. Jesse leaned against the door with his head on his arm as we followed the slow line of cars back through town. He looked awful low and sad, and I couldn't think of anything that would cheer him up. I hated to see him just go off down the road, with nothing to take with him and nowhere to go. In a minute I heard him singing the verse to the soldier song:

Far across th' dis-tant waters
Lived an ol' German's daughter,
On th' banks of th' ol' Rivah Rhiiinnne . . .

"Ain't that tune pretty?" he said. He looked out of the pickup window at the dark houses. We were

on the edge of town, then, and could see the yellow
lights of a big oil derrick, standing on the prairie
miles away.

"Fräulein, fräulein, look down from your window an' be mine," he sang. "That the way it goes?"
He sighed and slumped back in the seat. "I never
will forget that tune," he said.

I pulled in at Bill's, and we followed a group of
cowboys inside. When the last performance of the
rodeo was over, the people all left for another town,
so the café was almost empty, just a few tired rodeo
hands eating a late meal before starting their long
drives home. We took our pick of the booths. I
ordered coffee and cherry pie, and Jesse just ordered coffee. He went on talking.

"I knew this mornin' I was gonna do all this," he
said. He looked up and smiled when the ugly,
waddle-assed waitress set the coffee in front of him.
"I guess I done had it planned," he went on.
"Because I don't intend to ride in another arena
agin. Only reason I go to rodeos is to chase after the
prettiest tail I can find, and I know beforehand I
ain't gonna catch that." I ate my pie slowly, not
looking at him very often. He looked terrible, sick
and worn out, dark scraggly whiskers on his cheeks.
He kept nibbling at the tag of his Bull Durham
sack.

"Ain't no fräulein ever looked down on me," he
said. "Not unless it was to ask for money. Some
fellers just belong in whorehouses, I don't know
why."

"I halfway wish I was going someplace," I said. "I ain't doin' any good around here."

"You just think you ain't," he said. "You better stay till your Granddad gets back on his feet a little. That's a lot a good you can do. After he kinda gets over this it might not hurt you to see the world some."

"I don't know how long that will be," I said. "May not ever be. Granddad sure looks worn out." Somebody had put money in the jukebox. It was Ernest Tubb, singing "Rainbow at Midnight." His deep voice carried over what little talk there was in the café. The waitress was going around mopping off the dirty yellow tabletops with a dripping rag.

"You probably ain't got any money to leave on, anyway," Jesse said.

"Two hundred dollars calf money," I said. "That'd last me awhile."

"Yeah," he said, setting his coffee cup down. "About a week. But you're the boss." He rubbed his fingers into the corners of his eyes. "It don't hurt to take a little look around," he said. "Just don't turn into an old loose horse like me. You're better off to stop somewhere, even if it ain't no paradise. I could have myself, many a time. I had the chances any man has." He wiped his lips with his napkin, and dropped the napkin in his coffee cup. "I guess I was too particular, for too long, what's wrong with me. I went all over this cow country, looking for the exact right place an' the exact right people, so once I got stopped I wouldn't have to be movin' agin, like my old man always done. But that's going at it wrong. I shoulda just set down an' made it right wherever the hell it was.

"I ain't agoin' to now," he said, and he blew smoke out of his mouth with a weary breath.

"Granddad made something good," I said. "Look at him. It didn't stay made."

"Look at him," Jesse said, his voice sharp. "He lost something all right, but by god he's still got something too. I know a lot of people in worse situations than your granddad's in."

"Well, I guess he did make something he could keep," I said.

"I'd say so," Jesse said. "I'd say your granddad made it." His hands were clasped together on the table, and he looked shivery and shaky, like he'd just fallen in a cold winter river and pulled out to a place with no fire.

"Some folks do," he said.

CHAPTER

——————— 13 ———————

1.

Jesse had quit talking, and we sat listening to the jukebox. It was Wayne Rainey, singing

> Why don't you haul off
> And love me, like you
> Used to do . . .

Why do you treat me like a worn-out shoe, and on like that. My pie was eaten, except for a few crumbs, and I pushed them around with the red prongs of my fork. Finally Jesse got up. "Let's go," he said. "If you can run me back to the pens I'll find that truck and catch me a little nap."

He paid the ticket, and we went out. There were only five or six cars in the parking lot—one of them had its back doors open and a cowboy's legs stuck out one side. There were two or three beer cans under his heels. I drove Jesse back to the pens. The lights were out and the whole area was dark, but there were still a few cowboys around, sleeping in cars, or on blankets and sleeping bags spread behind the chutes. We found the truck, and I helped Jesse girt his saddle to the sideboards. He stood on the high running board, looking down at me.

"Well, I guess I better try an' snooze awhile," he said. "Much obliged for the ride an' all."

"Oh, you bet," I said. "You're welcome."

"Tell your grandpa I enjoyed working for him what little I did," he said. "I imagine I'll be running into you somewhere, one a these days."

"I hope you get a good job," I said.

"Oh, I guess I'll get by," he said. "It's hard times and dusty roads."

He said to be careful, and I said so long, Jesse. That's the last I'll ever see of him, I thought. I drove back through Thalia, under the fluttery rodeo flags that would have to come down for another year. The highway to the ranch was deserted, and all I could get on the radio was gospel singing and commercials from the station in Del Rio. I felt like I was losing people every day. If there had been anyplace open in Thalia besides Bill's, I would have gone back. A coyote ran across the road in front of me, yellow in the headlights, his eyes shining like marbles. I slammed on my brakes and grabbed for the thirty-thirty, but he had already scooted under the fence and disappeared.

2.

When I turned off at the cattle guard, I noticed a pair of headlights coming up behind me as fast as an ambulance. Before I had gone a half mile across the pasture the headlights were about a foot from my rear bumper, and I could see the Cadillac grille reflected in my rear-view mirror. Hud was right on my tail, and I started to pull to the right, so he could get by. But when I flashed my lights on bright I saw something. I saw somebody crawling and I was almost on him. Granddad! He was just in front of me, down on his hands and knees at the side of the road. I braked and swerved to the left and my car lights were right in his face and then they were on the empty road and the Cadillac jarred my rear end. Then I was bouncing over the left-hand bar ditch and into the pasture, the pick-up almost spinning over, so I was thrown against the far door and hung to the wheel with one hand, all the time seeing Granddad crawling toward me in his nightshirt, with blood on his chin. The high weeds and little mesquite bushes slowed the pickup enough that I stomped the pedals and got it stopped. I jumped out and ran back, but I didn't see Granddad. Hud was out in the road in front of his car, wiping blood off his nose. The grille of the Cadillac was caved in and one headlight broken, and Hud standing in the light of the other one slinging blood off his nose. For a minute I thought I had dreamed Granddad.

"Goddamn you," Hud said. "You little piss-ant. What the fuck did you stop for? You got your life's work ahead, paying for this car."

"No, didn't you see him?" I said. "He's out here, Granddad. He was crawlin' in the ditch."

"The hell he is," Hud said, turning toward the bar ditch. He threw a bloody handkerchief down, and in the stillness we heard Granddad say, "Jericho," real loud. He was in the ditch behind the car, still moving on his hands and knees. Hud knelt down and stopped him.

"Hud, who is it, hon?" Lily said. She was in the back seat.

"Oh, snakeshit," Hud said. "Run get that pickup an' point it this away, so we'll have light. I can't turn mine aroun' in this road. I may a run over him."

I ran to the pickup and backed it around, paying no attention to stumps or bushes. In the dark Granddad didn't look too bad hurt, and I wasn't quite as scared as I had been. I just couldn't figure it out. I turned off the pickup lights before I thought, but Hud yelled and I switched them back on. Hud was holding Granddad in his lap, trying to keep him from moving. All Granddad had on was his old nightshirt; he didn't even have shoes. But he recognized Hud.

"Don't hold me back, Huddie," he said. "I fell. I was going out to look at the cloud, see if it was time

211

to get the men up." His voice was hoarse and slow. "We got to get to work," he said. "Turn me loose now. I'm okay." I thought he was. I could see blood on his hands and knees, where the rocks and gravel had skinned him up, and there were grass burrs in his arms and in his nightshirt, but I thought he was all right. I thought he must have fallen off the porch or something and knocked himself silly, was all, like he might from a fall from a horse. But Hud wouldn't turn him loose, and when he wouldn't Granddad began to fight him, and to whine down in his throat.

"Lily," Hud yelled. "Lily, get up." Blood was dripping from Hud's smashed nose and dropping on Granddad and on his shirt.

"Annie, you help me," Granddad said. "Got to get up now and get these men started. Wake these men up. I can't lay here no more. A man ain't to crawl."

"Shit, this old man's hurt bad," Hud said. He lifted Granddad's nightshirt, and I suddenly saw a jagged end of bone protruding from Granddad's side above his hip. The sight made me turn weak.

"Lily, goddamnit, get up an' start that car," Hud said. He yelled at her and cussed her as loud as he could. Instead of starting it the woman got out and came around to us. When she saw Granddad she grabbed onto the fender of the Cadillac. She didn't have anything on from the waist up, nothing except a brown sweater she had pulled over her shoulders and buttoned in front. Her stomach was bare.

"Huddie, won't you let me up?" Granddad said. He was trying to get his hands loose; he was looking up at Hud, but he didn't see me. "It ain't no bad cloud," he said. "We got to get these men up an' get to work. Move stock." His voice was cracking, and he was whining when he breathed in air. Hearing the whine and seeing his throat jerk the way it did made tears come in my eyes. It seemed all of a sudden like Granddad was someone I had forgotten about for a long time, and hearing the deep hurt sound of his whine brought back all he was to me.

"Lie still, Granddad," I said. I couldn't think of any way to help. But Hud seemed to be thinking, he seemed to be in his right mind, and I just set there, holding Granddad's good leg still, waiting for Hud to decide what to do.

"Lily, take this car an' go to the house," he said. "Telephone's in the hall. Call for an ambulance and tell 'em to get here quick, the road through Bannon's horse pasture. Tell 'em we got an awful sick man. We'll try an' keep him quiet."

"Goddamn you, now don't hold a man down," Granddad said. His throat swelled, and he strained to get up. For a minute it was all the two of us could do to hold him, but then he went weak all of a sudden and lay back. All we could hear was him harking and coughing, and the Cadillac motor turning over.

"Knew it," Hud said. "Sonofabitch won't start no way. Five-thousand-dollar car, and it ain't no more use than a wagon. Ain't as much." I was on my knees, trying to pull some of the burrs out of Granddad's arms, but he wouldn't hold still. Hud was looking more wild-eyed and desperate, and Granddad just lay there weak, harking, and Hud's wrists were trembling as he held him still.

"Honey, I can't start it," Lily called. "The goddamn thing, I can't start it."

"Come on here," Hud yelled. "Bring that whiskey. It's in the seat." She came wobbling out on her high heels, the heavy bottle in one hand.

"See if we can get a little down him," Hud said. "Might help." I held Granddad's leg still, and Hud held his hands, and the woman squatted down and leaned over Granddad. She tried to tilt his head back and make him take some whiskey; but Granddad was trying to talk again, he was mumbling and trying to talk to the old people, to Grandmother and to Jericho Green, and the brownish whiskey bubbled off his mouth and ran in a stream down his chin and neck. It made a sharp smell, sharper than the dust smell of the road.

"Honey, I can't make him drink this stuff," the woman said. She had put her arms in the sleeves of the brown sweater, but it was loose in front and her breasts had fallen out. "I'm just wasting it, all I'm doin'," she said, and she kept trying to pour with one hand and hold the sweater together with the other, and I didn't like her for that.

"Keep pourin'," Hud said. "You're doin' all right." Finally Granddad took a little and gagged it up.

"You-all," he said. "You-all, don't make me drink that." Lily took the bottle away then and pressed her hands to her jaws, like she had the toothache.

"Look here," Hud said. "Yonder's a car coming out of Thalia. I just seen the lights up the road. Look now. Lonnie, he's a long ways up there yet. You run out to the road and flag him down, you can beat him. Tell him we got a dyin' man here. If he's got a big car make him come over, if he ain't make him telephone. Now hurry."

"I'm scared he'll die," I said. "He might while I'm gone. Can't we take him in the pickup some way?"

"Get on, or I'll promise you he'll die," Hud said, frowning at me. Blood from his nose had dripped and smeared all over the lower part of his face, and he looked terrible.

"He's sufferin' agony," Hud said. "You stop that car."

3.

I ran down the dark dirt road as fast as I could, fighting the darkness with my arms and legs. Hud had said Granddad was dying, and I could remember the bone tip protruding from his side. The darkness shut in around me, and two or three times I ran off in the brush and weeds, stumbling into the bar ditch and out again on the soft, graded road. I began to give out in the legs, and I had to slow down, but anyway I got across the cattle guard and onto the pavement with the car still a good mile up the road toward Thalia. I stood at the edge of the pavement and waited, the longest wait, and the lights came on toward me. They disappeared beneath some little ridge, and then came in sight again and the car swept down the slope my way. I got in the middle of the road and waved my hands and hat, and the man hit his brakes. It was a big Olds, and I was thinking we could load Granddad into the back seat and take him to the hospital in it. The driver kept slowing down, and I stepped off the road so I could talk to him. But the minute I did the motor roared and the car went zooming by, the fender just under my elbow in the dark. The man who was driving wasn't even looking at me. I yelled for help, but by that time he was gone, doing sixty or seventy miles an hour. I guess he was afraid I'd hijack him.

And then I was alone, standing on the edge of the pavement in the darkness, thinking of how Granddad was hurting, how he had whined. Hud said he was suffering agony. I walked up and down the highway, I don't know how many minutes, trying to think of something I could do. I knew I ought to do something. I looked for another set of headlights, anywhere, in any direction, but none were in sight. It was between two and three o'clock, about the deadest hour of the night, and I knew there might not be another car along for half an hour. I wished I had run the other way, to the ranch house. It would have been farther, but there was a telephone there, at least. That hadn't occurred to me in time, and it hadn't occurred to Hud either. I wanted to start back. It seemed like I had been gone for an hour, and that Granddad might be a lot sicker, might even be dying. Or Hud might have decided to try and move him in the pickup after all. I was walking around on the pavement, my head down, and when I looked up I almost hollered. I saw another car, another set of lights coming from Thalia. It was a good ways off, but I got in the middle of the road and waited. If the car got by it would have to run right over me, or else go into the bar ditch, and I would have a chance to yell. The lights were only a few hills away, and I was hoping it would be another big car, big enough to move Granddad in. Then I looked up the road, and the lights weren't coming. I walked a little ways up the road while I waited for them to come over the ridge, and they didn't come. I walked and waited till I knew there wasn't a chance. The car must have turned off; it must have been somebody from Thalia going home. Or else the driver just pulled off the road to go to sleep. I was almost sick at my stomach from waiting and walking the highway and worrying about Granddad. I looked toward the pastures, and I could see the faint light above the mesquites, the pickup lights. It seemed out of place, and I looked again and discovered I had walked nearly a half mile up the road from the cattle guard. Seeing the lights made me think of Hud and Granddad, there in the bar ditch all that time, Hud wild, and Granddad suffering and dying, and the butter-haired woman with her breasts hanging out of the sweater. I began to run back, to run down the pavement toward the cattle guard. When I got there I stopped just a minute, to take one last good look up and down the highway. But I didn't see any lights, and I went on to the cattle guard. I was going across it when I heard a woman's voice, pretty faint, but like a yell, and then a bang, a gun shot, and the long cracking echo off Idiot Ridge. It could have been the Cadillac starting; it could have been a backfire. But the sound and the echo had been too much like sounds I had heard before, and I remembered the coyote gun. After I saw the coyote, I hadn't taken time to put it back behind the seat. I remembered trying to keep it from bouncing off when Hud had knocked the pickup across the road.

I left the cattle guard and started back, but I went slow, like I had gone to Halmea's cabin that last night. Before I got very far I could hear the roar of a big truck coming toward Thalia. It was far away, miles away maybe. I walked on toward the one shadowy spot of light in the mesquite. I didn't know what to think at first. Then I thought Hud must of shot the woman; he must have killed her for some reason. That was why she screamed. And then I knew he wouldn't shoot her, and I thought it must have been Truman Peters. Truman must have been waiting for Hud at the ranch. He must have seen the light and come down the road and found them, seen his wife with her naked teats and Hud had had to shoot him. I knew he couldn't shoot Hud. I got scared and began to walk faster. I wanted to be out in the light. Then I heard the woman crying something at Hud, and I didn't hear anything else.

4.

When I came into the light, Lily was bent over the turtleback of the big car, crying into her elbow. Hud stood by the fender of the pickup, talking to himself. The bottle of whiskey was sitting on the fender, and the rifle leaned against the pickup door. I saw the ejected shell laying in the dirt road, the brass shining in the light. Hud was talking, to himself, or to Lily, I never did know. Then he drank, his head jerking quickly back.

My granddad lay in the bar ditch. He lay still. An old Levi jacket, the one we kept behind the pickup seat, it had been thrown over his face, so I couldn't see what he looked like, or see his head at all. Lily's dress, the fancy one all white and gold, was stretched over Granddad too; it covered up his side. Just his two bare legs stuck out from under the dress, one straight, and one bent crooked, and scarred up besides from that rope tear years and years before. I knew it was Granddad there dead, but I kept thinking it wasn't. I saw some blood puddled in the gravel by the Levi jacket, and I choked and gagged. But I didn't get sick. I went over and squatted down by Granddad, by the good leg I had tried to hold. Seeing the Levi jacket over his face made me remember all the things I had meant to buy him and give him, sometime or other. I had meant to buy him a blanket-lined jacket, for one thing.

I heard a whiz. Hud's arm swung. There was a whistle, and the whiskey bottle hit the ground somewhere in the pasture. "Whiskey, ain't it," Hud said. His voice wasn't loud. I saw there were still grass burrs in Granddad's legs. In a minute I felt Hud come and stand behind me. I couldn't feel any of Granddad there with us; it was just Hud and me. I looked up at him and he was looking off into the dark. I felt like I would gag again, but inside I was all dry and hot, like I had fever. Hud was looking into the pickup headlights, stretching his hands out toward them like the lights were a fire and it was winter.

"Lonnie," he said. "No shit, it was the best thing. The pore old worn-out bastard."

"But he woulda been," I said. "It woulda been all right, he woulda got well. I needed him." I started to pull the jacket off and look at Granddad's face, but I didn't. Hud came around in front of me and squatted down. I knew he wanted me to listen to him. He looked right at me, and didn't do it to scare. I saw sweat on his cheeks, but his voice seemed easy for once, not mean or rough.

"You listen to me," he said. "No shit, it was best. I ain't lyin' now. Homer wanted it."

"But he wasn't so bad," I said. That was all I could say. If I could have felt Granddad was there, I could have felt something to say. But it was just Hud and me.

"Hell, I had to," he said. "He was bad off, Lonnie. You wasn't here. You wasn't acoming, and he got to spittin' blood and tryin' to get up, an' hurtin' himself. Tryin' to get to them goddamn dead people a his. I thought if he wanted to get to 'em so bad I'd just let him go. He always liked them better than us that was alive, anyhow."

"But he was Granddad," I said.

"He was all fucked up," Hud said. "He was throwin' up blood, and that leg like it was. Worse than it was the first time he hurt it. He was just an old worn-out bastard. He couldn't a made it up no way in the world. He couldn't a made it another hour."

Then Lily come over an' hung on Hud's shoulders, mumbling something about Truman in his ear. But he didn't even look around at her; he was still talking to me.

"But what will I do?" I said. "Granddad was always . . ."

"You'll do without, like the rest of us," he said. "Lonnie, no shit now, he was ruined. He wasn't ever gonna be no good agin, he was just gonna lay somewhere an' rot. I took an' shot him cause he needed me to."

"Honey, don't just squat there talkin'," Lily said. She was trying to get Hud to stand up. "Hud, put him in the car," she said. "Let's go let people know. Somebody's gonna come along."

I just squatted there, looking at the Levi jacket and the stickers in his legs, and trying to feel something of Granddad, so I'd know something to do. I saw Hud looking down at Granddad too. Only Hud looked easy and peaceful someway, like he was finally satisfied for the first time in his life.

"You don't know the story," he said. "Me and him fought many and many a round, me and Homer Bannon. It's hard to say, though. I helped him as much as he ever helped me, I believe that."

I dried up then. I felt like I didn't have anything else to say, to Hud or anybody, ever. I wasn't down on Hud. I didn't even think about him. I was just pushed back in myself like a two-bit variety-store telescope.

Finally Hud stood up and told the woman to get in the pickup. Then he went over and put the gun behind the seat, where it belonged.

"You take his feet," he said, when he came back. "Let's lay him on the wagon sheet. It ain't gonna hurt him none now. We can take him on to the hospital; maybe they'll clean him up a little."

"Don't they have to see it?" I said. "The sheriff and the law?"

Hud kinda smiled, and shook his head. "If they won't take it the way we tell 'em, let 'em do without," he said. "Ain't nobody gonna lie." He grinned his old, strange grin, and I didn't know at all. I had believed him. I thought at first that he shot

222

Granddad to stop the hurting. But seeing that wild blood-smeared grin, I didn't know. It could have been for kindness or for meanness either, whichever mood was on Hud when he held Granddad in the ditch.

We lifted Granddad and laid him in the back of the pickup, on the wagon sheet I had used when I listened to those songs. Hud made me drive, and he sat back there and held Granddad from bumping till I could get to Thalia. And when the hospital had took Granddad away, Hud made me drive Lily to the hotel, so she could get some sleep, and he borrowed a car from one of the doctors and went and woke up the sheriff and the justice of the peace and told them about it.

CHAPTER

14

1.

All the next day I sat in the barn loft, thinking and trying to figure things out. Some of the people from Thalia came down to the lots to look for me, but I kept quiet, and none of them thought to climb the ladder. I knew they had found the place where Granddad fell off the porch and hurt himself. So anyway, that part of it was settled. The high loft door was open, and I could watch the people around the house come and go, like they did all day long. I sat with my back against some bales of alfalfa and looked out the loft door at the sky. There must have been at least a thousand white clouds that crossed the sky that day. I wasn't crying or hurting or worrying much. I was just watching the people and the thunderclouds. Once in a great while I would wonder where Granddad was. I would wonder if there was any part of him watching it all from someplace. I had heard the song about the ghost riders, and I wondered if there could be anything of Granddad riding that big sky, in the thickets of cloud. Sometimes I felt for a minute like there might be, and other times I thought it was a silly thing to think.

There were a couple of police cars around the house most of the day. I saw the deputy sheriff out in the back yard looking around a time or two, but he didn't come to the barn. Late in the afternoon Hud and Lily and Grandma came out on the back porch and stood awhile, and then Hud and Lily got in the Cadillac and drove away. The Cadillac's grille was still all mashed in, but Hud had managed to get it running. Hud looked okay, and he acted like he was running things. I tried to decide for myself why he really killed Granddad, but I couldn't. I never could tell why Hud did things; he was too much a mystery to me. But I could sure tell that he was in control, and that Truman Peters, or the law, or anybody else wasn't going to get him stopped for a while. I knew they'd probably have some kind of a trial about Granddad's killing, but they wouldn't give Hud much trouble. I had watched a good many trials in Thalia, and I'd seen a lot dumber people than Hud get away with doing a lot worse things than he had done. Even if they hung a sentence on him it would be suspended. With Granddad gone, nobody would slow Hud down.

During the heat of the day the loft was like an oven, and I had to sneak down to the water tank a time or two to drink. Finally I wet my shirt and spread it under me for a pallet, but I didn't go to sleep. Cars kept driving up to the house, and I watched the people go in. Most of them were womenfolks, bringing things to eat. Later in the afternoon, when it began to cool off, they really came thick, and a lot of people were milling around in the back yard. The sky was the same big sky I had always known, the same blues and whites and grays, and the same hawks circling around in it. About dark I climbed down and went to the house. The people tried to make a fuss over me, but I told them I didn't feel good, and I went to my room and changed clothes. There were piles of food in the kitchen, and I was hungry, so I went back down and ate a little. It turned out the food was mostly cakes and potato salad. Nobody paid much attention to me, because a carload of Granny's kinfolk had come in about that time. When I was full, I slipped out of the back door and left in the pickup.

It was Halmea I wanted to talk to, and I drove to her house first. I felt like Halmea would have heard all about it, and would be waiting for me to come and talk. When I drove up to the house there were a few colored boys and a couple of girls standing in the street. They were laughing and hugging themselves and pushing each other around for the fun of it. I saw one girl who was Halmea's friend. It seems like her name was Eunice. I went over to them and they all quit laughing, and I asked them if they knew where I could find Halmea.

"You too late," Eunice said. "She done left fo' Dee-troit. She been gone since yesterdy."

"Already left?" I said. I felt silly and disappointed. It was an awful letdown, and for a minute I didn't know what to say.

"She tol' me you'd be comin' aroun'," the girl said. "But she didn't say why she goin', and she didn't leave no 'dress with me. You might get it from Aunt Beulah."

But the address wouldn't have given me what I wanted, and I didn't waste any time trying to explain it all to the old deaf woman who was rocking on the porch. If Halmea was gone, they were all gone, and Thalia might as well be empty. I was so disappointed I almost turned around and went back home, but finally I drove down to Hermy's. I thought there might at least be some news about him. Sometimes rodeo performers aren't hurt as bad as it looks like at first, and I thought he might even be home from the hospital.

Hermy's little sister met me at the door. She said her folks were still at the hospital, and that she'd been left at home with the littlest kids. She was about sixteen, and her name was Grace. I had dated her once or twice, but I'd known her so long, and Hermy and I were such close buddies, that we didn't accomplish much together. She said she didn't know anything. She thought Hermy was still pretty bad off. I found out which hospital he was in, and left. I meant to go see him as soon as I could get away. When I left Hermy's house I went downtown and made the square a time or two, but it was Sunday night, and only one night after the rodeo, and nobody was there but old Buttermilk and his dog. I began to feel like I was the only person left in the country, and it was a shitty feeling. On my way home, though, I stopped in at Bill's a minute for a hamburger and ran into Buddy Andrews and another kid or two, and we sat around and fed the jukebox until it was pretty late.

2.

There didn't seem to be a soul there when I came up to the church, and that suited me fine. It was Monday afternoon, right in the hottest part of the day. I had taken all I could stand of Grandma and her kinfolks, and once I was dressed up there wasn't anyplace to go but to the church house. When I saw there wasn't any cars parked out in front I felt better, and I hurried up the steps. Inside it would at least be cool and quiet and peaceful, not like the ranch house.

But when I opened the doors I saw that I had been mistaken. They must have just driven the hearse away to gas it up. I stood inside, on the thick carpet, and the black coffin set right in front of me, below the pulpit. I didn't want to sit in the family section that they had marked off with blue ribbon, so I sat down close to the back. I picked up a songbook to hold in my hands.

Two of the funeral people were there waiting: the

man from the home, and Old Lady Singer, who played the piano. The minute I sat down Old Lady Singer began to play "Abide with Me," and she kept on playing it for hours it seemed like, all the time the people were coming in. The piano didn't sound too well in tune, and the old lady wasn't too good at playing it, either. I squeezed the songbook in my hand and made it bend. The man from the funeral home was one of the sorriest shits I had ever seen. Watching him, I wasn't so sad, not even with the sorrowful music the old lady was playing. He made me feel cold, and scornful, I guess. I had seen him the day before at the house, late in the afternoon. He had been whining around Granny about providence, when all he wanted was to get both hands in somebody's pocket. He was really spruced up for the big occasion, wearing a tar-paper-black suit and black shoes with flashy wing tips. There were a lot of big springy piles of flowers around the coffin, and he was arranging them. Once in a while he sneaked a glance at me or the old lady, to see if we appreciated his labor. The little black button of his hearing aid stuck on the side of his head like a woman's earring. I wanted to go up and see Granddad someway and have my good-by over with, but all I could do was listen to the sorrowful music, and squeeze the songbook. I squeezed it and squeezed it until I thought the notes would drip out and splash on the floor.

But anyhow, it was dark in the church, and the deep-blue glass windows were cool as shady water. I always liked those blue windows, and I liked the rich brown wood of the church seats, wood that was the color of Halmea's breasts. But they had a sweety-sweet picture of Jesus over the choir booths that I didn't like at all. Jesus looked like he was a Boy Scout, waiting to get his twenty-first merit badge from the head Scout Master.

I was trying to decide to leave, when the people began to come through the church doors. A world of ranch people came. The bosses were there from all the headquarters, and a lot of hired hands with them, and a few that were just loose cowboys. A good many of them had worked for Granddad at one time or another, and nearly all of them had worked with him. Then the old ladies from Thalia trooped in, whispering to one another and shaking powder on the aisles. I could hear them whispering how Granddad had gone to a better place. They could think so and go to hell; I didn't believe it. Not unless dirt is a better place than air. I could see Granddad in my mind a thousand ways, but always he was on the ranch doing something, he wasn't in any loaf-around eternal life. I could see him riding, enjoying his good horses; or I could see him tending the cattle; or see him just standing in the grass, looking at the land and trying to figure out ways to beat the dry weather and the wind. Those were good places to me, and any one of them was a damn sight better than being in a church house, in a coffin, with a chicken-shit snooping around you and a lot of old ladies talking. They could talk Bible till they were blue in the face, and end up dirt too someday. The longer I sat and watched it—the man, the old ladies, the little girls coming in fluffed up like cotton candy—the colder I got, and the worse I hated it all. More people came than Granddad would ever have dreamed of having: store people and businessmen and oil drillers and strangers by the swarm. People were at the funeral that Granddad hadn't ever seen. Some were there that he'd forgotten, and some that he hated and despised. Their wives were with them, all wearing slick black dresses, with little veils hanging down over their eyes and white gloves on their hands. In a little while the whole church was full, except for the two rows they saved for Grandma and her people. The funeral-home man put some of the late ones to bringing in chairs from the Sunday-school rooms, so they could fill the aisles.

Finally I saw Grandma and one of her sisters go by, and I knew it was fixing to start. Grandma didn't look at me. Then somebody took hold of my arm, and I saw Hud. He was wearing a new, expensive-looking suit, and a necktie with it.

"You come on," he said. "You got to sit with us."

I didn't want to move, so I didn't say anything. But Hud squeezed my arm till I felt his fingers pinching the bone, and I knew I had to go or be dragged. I got up, but I kept the songbook in my hand.

He sat me down so close to the front that I could see the glass cover of the coffin, and the satin padding around the inside rim. Seeing it made me feel weak. Two of the ladies on the row behind me were sniffling, and hearing them made me cold again.

Then Old Lady Singer stopped playing for a minute. When she did, the choir trailed in, and the two preachers right behind them. One of the preachers was Brother Barstow, and the other one I didn't know. They sat down without saying a word. Then the choir got up again, and began to sing "Rock of Ages." When they got to the line about the water and the blood I began to shiver, and I couldn't stop myself.

When the song was finished, the preacher I didn't know got up and went to the pulpit. He leaned on it for a long time and looked down at us without saying anything. He took his handkerchief out of his coat pocket, and I thought he was going to cry like the old ladies. But he just cleaned his glasses. When he got them clean, he fished a little card out of his pocket and began to read about Granddad.

He read his name to be Homer Lisle Bannon—born in Texas in 1868, and died there 1954. Died the last day of July. He told how Granddad had come to the Panhandle when he was just a boy, and how he had been a cowboy and a cattleman all his life. He told about him marrying my real grandmother, and when she died; and he told about when my daddy was born, and when he died; and he told about Granddad marrying Grandma, and he mentioned me. Then he went on and told a lot that wasn't true, about Granddad and the church. He told some more that wasn't true about Granddad's being respected and loved by people all over the state. There wasn't hardly anybody cared much for Granddad. Some liked him and some were scared of him and a good many hated his guts. Me and a few cowmen and a few hands and an old-timer or two loved and respected him some.

Hud hadn't changed expression the whole time, but Grandma had quit sniffling and was sitting up looking proud. The tears had rutted out the powder on her cheeks until her face looked like wet plaster. Then Mrs. Turner, the lady who sang the high parts for the choir, came down to the piano to sing a solo. She sang solos for everything, but she practiced her singing, and was good at it. The song she sang was "Yes, We'll Gather at the River," and she sang it too fine for me to stay cold. Yes, she sung, we'll gather at the river, the beautiful, the beautiful river. She sang out, and I could see the cords quivering in her throat. While she was singing I wasn't mad, and my eyes got hot and I had to wipe the wetness away with my fingers. She made the song go higher and higher, and as long as it lasted everything was different, and I thought again that Granddad might be moving above the pastures. I saw the river, running down the canyon and out under the trees, with cattle standing in it, and horses watering at the pools. It was a sight Granddad always loved, a flowing river. But Mrs. Turner finished too soon, and sat down, and I knew she wouldn't sing any more by herself. I lost the river, and heard the women sniffling, and I knew Granddad was done with flowing water for good and all.

Brother Barstow got up, then, to do the sermon, and I got dry quick. Brother Barstow was Grandma's crony, and Granddad's mortal enemy. He was a big man, proud as a peafowl, always gossiping with widow women, and trying to get something on everybody, just in case. Grandma used to have him out to the ranch a lot, to devil Granddad. The first time he came, Granddad was polite enough, but he told the preacher plain as day that he had got along without churches for a good long while, and that he didn't intend to start with them so late. Then one day Brother Barstow came out, during a revival week, and tried to get Granddad to say he'd go with Jesus. He didn't explain where. Granddad thought it was ignorant talk, and told him so. But Brother Barstow kept on about it till he made Granddad mad, and Granddad run him off. Granny had him back, but after that Granddad stayed out of his way.

When he got to the pulpit he took out his handkerchief and wiped his forehead and his eyes. Then he looked up at the ceiling, and stuck the handkerchief back in his pocket. "Let us pray," he said.

"Our dear Heavenly Father," he said. "One of our beloved neighbors has been called up to dwell with Thee. We that are left here with our anguish and loss pray that You will receive him into Glory, and feast him, and keep him in Your holy Love, throughout Eternity. Homer Bannon was one of Your faithful servants. He was a herdsman, and he tended his flocks and Yours well; and we know that You will grant him his reward. We bow our heads to You, oh God, and put our trust in Thy love and Thy mercy. And we won't fear for Homer Bannon, because we know he is with You. But for those of you Your children who must remain longer in this place of trials and sorrows, we pray You will send strength. We pray that You will plant Your rod, that we may lean on it and grow strong, so that when the day comes for us to lay down our earthly husks, as Brother Homer has, we may come humbly and penitent to Thee. Be with us now, and give us courage, as we ask these things in the name of Thy son our Lord, Jesus Christ. Amen."

Granny and her kinfolks and the old ladies were crying like they were all about to die, and Brother Barstow stood looking down at them, calm and shiny-eyed, like they were just little kids with skint knees. He waited till they got a little quieter, and then he began to turn through his Bible. He acted like he had lost his place, and he kept turning pages, looking for it. Then-all he found the place he wanted, and he bent over it and nodded. The people got quiet, and he raised his head and popped the Bible shut.

"Good people," he said, "we have gathered here in this holy place today to mourn the closing of another great book of life. Brother Homer Bannon, whom we all knew and loved, has at last been called to his rest." Hud leaned over then and whispered in my ear—it was the only time he moved during the whole sermon. "Called, my ass," he said. "It looked to me like he was driven."

Brother Barstow went right on.

"As his good friend and pastor, I knew Homer Bannon well, and in his declining years I visited him often. We grew to know one another, and as our friendship ripened, Homer and I often sat and talked about the day when he would be going to his reward.

"And so, my friends, my own heart was as grieved as yours to hear of Homer's passing. This morning it grieved me so that I couldn't sleep. I got out of bed and went out on my porch, and I watched the night turn to morning. And when I saw God's sun come up, when I saw it shed the message of His glory over the world, I thought of Homer Bannon, and I was reassured."

He stood there a minute, solemn, and he opened his Bible and began to read. I wished I could have laughed out loud at all he said. I wish I could have laughed and laughed and laughed. Or I wish Hud would have done it. But we didn't.

"In the Book of Genesis, Fifth Chapter, Twenty-fourth verse, it says: 'And Enoch walked with God; and he was not; for God took him.'" He closed the Bible again and leaned on it with his elbow.

"And friends, that is how it was with Homer Bannon," he said. "He walked with God, and God took him. Homer raised his horses and his cattle on God's earth. He watched over them like a good shepherd, and because he did, God made his life a Glory.

"Homer was a friend to God, and God gave him a long life. He gave him material abundance, and He gave him a loving family to watch over him in the days of his feebleness. And now God has taken him, taken him where he will never have to labor in the sun and the sleet again. He has taken him to a range it is not ours to trod, where the grass withereth not, and neither does the water fail. Homer made a date with God, an appointment, and he kept it. Many's the time, before the days of his infirmities, when I have seen Homer Bannon riding out to tend his herds, and I have thought: 'There is a good man. There is a man for God.' And now, he has not perished, he has merely kept his contract with God, and ridden on. And we who are left have a contract with God also, and if we follow Homer's example we will someday be granted our appointment. When that appointment comes, when we get to that place, that land beyond the river, richer than even this land, finer than even this land, we will find our friend Homer Bannon there ahead of us, ranging on Eternity. 'And Enoch walked with God; and he was not; for God took him.' "

When he finished my legs were jerking. I was thinking of how Granddad really did feel about land, how he was always studying it. A lot of people

in the church were crying. As soon as Brother
Barstow sat down, the choir got up again and sang
"Whispering Hope." Mrs. Turner sang high and
splendid all the way through it, and I was shivery
again. Then Brother Barstow got back up and said:
"Now dear people may the grace of our Lord and
Saviour Jesus Christ rest and abide with each now
and forevermore, Amen." In a minute the pallbearers came down to the front and stood there looking
awkward while the funeral-home man fiddled with
the coffin. He made them all stand back, so he
could be the center of attention for a while. Then
they picked the coffin up and carried it toward the
back of the church, and I thought they were taking
it away. The funeral man came over and stood by
Grandma and motioned for us to stay seated. "The
mourners are looking now," he said. I looked
around and saw the coffin sitting right in the door
of the church. I saw a man lifting his little girl up, so
she could see Granddad.

Then the man motioned for us to get up, and I
followed Hud out of the aisle. I could see the coffin
again, and it seemed as big as a boat. It was much
too big for Granddad. He was just skin and bones.
The silver rim around the coffin shone like fire, and
when I got closer I saw that all the inside of it was
lined with pink satin. Granddad was laying there in
it, what was left of him. He had never been in
anything as showy as that before. I stopped by the
side of it, and then I knew that he was really dead
and gone forever; I may not have known it before.

They had a slick black suit on him, and a white shirt and a vest, and a dark red necktie with a little gold bird on it. His hands were on his chest, as white as paint. I squeezed the songbook when I looked at his face. They had put paint on him, like a woman wears, red paint. I could see it on his cheeks, and caked around his mouth. I could see slick oil on his hair, and some sticky stuff like honey around his eyes. I wished I could have buried him like he died; he was better that way. I stood there too long, I didn't want to move away from him, and finally Hud pulled me a step or two. He held my arm.

"Come on," he said. "Let 'em take him to the graveyard an' put him down. Let's get this shit over with." I went with him to the edge of the people, and we stood there while Grandma looked. She was the last one. Then the man shut the lid so nobody could see, and I was glad. The pallbearers lifted the coffin and set it in the back of the hearse.

"Come on," Hud said. "You got to ride with us to the graveyard."

But before he got hold of me I turned and jumped back into the people. I slipped through them and got clear and ran way around to the back of the church. I wasn't going any farther with that crowd, Hud or no Hud. He didn't seem to be following me, and I fell on the ground behind a hedge.

Then I heard the cars begin to drive off. The church got quiet, and I sat there in my good clothes, on the ground. I felt like crying a little then, because the day was so bad, because they had finally hit at Granddad when he couldn't hit back. But my eyes were dry, and I was hot as if I had fever.

I opened the songbook and began to look for the song about the beautiful river, but I couldn't find it. I hummed a little of it to myself, and then I remembered how Mrs. Turner sang it, how fine it sounded when she sang the words about the beautiful, the beautiful river. It made me remember Granddad, like he was before the cattle sickness, in those days when he had some laughing in him. I remembered a lot of things about him that I hadn't thought of in a long time: how I used to sneak out of bed early in the mornings and watch out the window as he passed by on his way to the pasture, the wild cowboys following behind. I was always wondering what horse he would take—he might take a bronc or not. Once after he'd been sick he made the cowboys wire him on with baling wire, so he wouldn't get weak and fall. I looked down at the bare ground behind the hedge, the bare brown ground, and I remembered that they had taken Granddad to put him in it. I guess he had passed me finally and for good, to go to his land. It began to seem like they hadn't hurt him so much, after all—anyway, he had stayed with the land, like he always intended to do. The coffin and the paint wouldn't matter once he was deep in the land. I decided then that I wouldn't need to worry a lot about keeping his ranch, or about losing it, either, because whatever I did about it would just be for me. He had always held the land, and would go on holding what he needed of it forever. I got up then and walked around to the front of the church, looking at the green grass on the ground, and watching the white clouds ease into the sky from the south. I went in the church and laid the songbook on a seat. Then I went back outside and stood on the walk in front of the church house, looking at the grass, at the skim-milk clouds, at those blue church-house windows, thinking of the horseman that had passed.

EPILOGUE

The next afternoon I left Thalia, and nobody but Hud knew I was going. I told him I wanted to go visit Hermy, and that I might go somewhere else and work awhile if I could happen onto a job. He said it would be all right with him, but that they'd probably want me to come back when all the legal business about the killing came up. He said that might be a good while. Hud seemed calm and fairly friendly, and he didn't act depressed at all. They were going to try to indict him for murder without malice, but he said he didn't think they'd ever do it. The worst he could get if they did was five years, and that was nearly always suspended. I knew he'd probably come out of it on top. He told me to keep in touch, so they could locate me in a hurry if they needed me.

I took a few clothes and a few of my paperbacks and drove to town in the pickup. I drew my money out of the bank, and left the pickup parked in front of the courthouse, where Hud could find it easy. But it was the middle of the afternoon and hot as fire, and I didn't feel like just striking off down the highway. I fiddled around the drugstore awhile, and then went to the pool hall and shot snooker till almost dark. I even won about six bits. When I came out it was dusk, and the four street lights around the square were lit. I stood on the curb by the pickup. They had sprinkled the courthouse lawn, and the water and grass and hot day made a good smell. I got my suitcase and decided to make a start. A red cattle truck was stopped by the filling station, and the driver was out checking his tires. I walked over and stood watching him.

"Felt like I had a flat," he said, coming around the truck. He grinned at me. "Guess I'm feeling things."

"Where you headed?" I asked. I felt a little silly.

"Raton, New Mexico," he said. "Goin' all the way, an' comin' back through here sometime tomorrow night. I truck outa Fort Worth."

"Could you let me ride to Wichita?" I said. "I got to get there tonight."

"Why sure, hell yes," he said. He was a short blackheaded guy with a pot belly and a crazy grin. He waved for me to get in the truck. "I been lonesome as a hound-dog all the way," he said. "My name's Bobby Don Brewer."

I crawled up in the high, bouncy cab, and set my suitcase between my legs. "I'm Lonnie Bannon," I said, and we shook hands. "A buddy of mine got hurt bull-ridin' the other night, an' I thought I'd go see him."

Bobby Don ground the truck in gear and we

started off. "I used to ride them bulls when I was a young fucker," he said, spitting out the window. "But I got me two boys now. Mama don't let me rodeo no more. Sometimes I miss it, you know." He slapped the seat with his hand, and honked at a gasoline truck, looking a little saddened. "I had me some good times, rodeoing," he said. "Runnin' aroun', drinkin' beer an' all that. Knew some good ol' boys I don't get to see no more. All of us out scratchin' for a livin', I guess."

"Say?" he said. "Bannon, you say? Kin to Homer Bannon?"

"I'm his grandson," I said. "You know him?"

"Hell, yes, I know him," he said. "I trucked many a head a cattle off his ranch. Hell, I remember you now, remember seeing you. How is Mister Homer?"

I didn't want to get in a long conversation about it.

"Mean as he ever was," I said.

He grew quiet, and we rode through the outskirts of Thalia. The sun was going into the great western canyons, the cattleland was growing dark. I saw the road and the big sky melt together in the north, above the rope of highway. I was tempted to do like Jesse once said: to lean back and let the truck take me as far as it was going. But I wanted to see Hermy, and I knew Bobby Don wouldn't have any time to waste. I saw the lights of houses as we flashed by in the darkness, the little houses, the ranches and the farms I knew. Bobby Don hummed some old song whose tune I had forgotten, and I sat thinking about Thalia, making the rounds in my mind. At *home it was time for the train to go by, and nobody was sitting on the porch. But for a little while, as the truck rolled on across the darkened range, I had them all, those faces who made my days: Jesse and Granddad, Halmea and Hud.*

"Goddamn," Bobby Don said, turning to me. "It's sure too bad about your buddy gettin' hurt. Them bulls can be bad business, I know that."

The cab was dark and the dash light threw shadows across his face, so that when I looked at him, and saw him pull down his old straw hat and face the road, he reminded me of someone that I cared for, he reminded me of everyone I knew.

COMING IN
JUNE 1992
FROM
SIMON & SCHUSTER

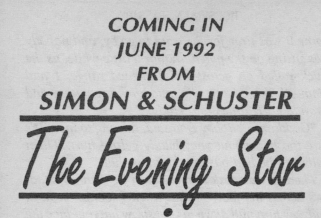

The Evening Star

•

Is McMurtry at his best—
He brings us up to date on
one of his most beloved novels
Terms of Endearment,
and on one of his most
memorable characters
Aurora Greenway
and her family, friends, and lovers
in this richly imagined
and satisfying tale.

•

Available Wherever
Hardcovers Are Sold

The Pulitzer
Prize-Winning
Masterpiece!

LONESOME DOVE

Larry McMurtry

POCKET
BOOKS

Available from Pocket Books

LARRY McMURTRY

THE PULITZER
PRIZE-WINNING
AUTHOR OF
LONESOME DOVE

☐ **BUFFALO GIRLS**
   73527-6/$5.99

☐ **LONESOME DOVE**
   68390-X/$6.99

☐ **TEXASVILLE**
   73517-9/$5.95

☐ **SOMEBODY'S DARLING**
   74585-9/$5.95

☐ **MOVING ON**
   74408-9/$6.95

☐ **THE DESERT ROSE**
   72763-X/$4.95

☐ **CADILLAC JACK**
   73902-6/$5.99

☐ **ANYTHING FOR BILLY**
   74605-7/$5.95

☐ **SOME CAN WHISTLE**
   72213-1/$5.99

POCKET
BOOKS

Simon & Schuster Mail Order Dept. LSS
200 Old Tappan Rd., Old Tappan, N.J. 07675

Please send me the books I have checked above. I am enclosing $_____ (please add 75¢ to cover
postage and handling for each order. Please add appropriate local sales tax). Send check or money
order—no cash or C.O.D.'s please. Allow up to six weeks for delivery. For purchases over $10.00 you
may use VISA: card number, expiration date and customer signature must be included.

Name _____

Address _____

City _____ State/Zip _____

VISA Card No. _____ Exp. Date _____

Signature _____ 151-21